ISBN 978-1-332-40250-2
PIBN 10422349

ANNOTATED ENGLISH TRANSLATION OF URDŪ ROZ-MARRA OR "EVERY-DAY URDU" THE TEXT-BOOK FOR THE LOWER STANDARD EXAMINATION IN HINDUSTANI

BY

LIEUT.-COLONEL D. C. PHILLOTT, F.A.S.B.,

Secretary and Member, Board of Examiners; Fellow of the Calcutta University; Author of Hindustani Manual, Hindustani Stumbling-Blocks, etc., etc.

CALCUTTA:

PRINTED AT THE BAPTIST MISSION PRESS.

1911.

INTRODUCTION.

The present translation has purposely been made not literal, except in places. Literal translations have indeed their special uses, but to the ordinary beginner they usually do more harm than good. Translation consists in expressing the thought and idiom of one language in the thought and idiom of another. A literal translation into Hindustani of "I missed the train" is obviously absurd, yet every month candidates are guilty of even greater absurdities. An authority has, indeed, stated that 'a paraphrase is not a translation,' but this much-quoted statement is probably capable of explanation. If it is desired to express "red as a lobster" in Hindustani, the phrase should be paraphrased by "red as a beet-root," which is a good Hindustani idiom. Were, however, a coarser English expression used, it would be better to translate it by its Hindustani equivalent *bandar sā lāl*, though the former paraphrase would not be incorrect. Such niceties of translation are, of course, not expected from Lower and Higher Standard candidates; but it is as well to have a standard of perfection even though one may not attain to it oneself.

A translation, as well as the orginal text-book, should be used intelligently. The text-book should be read through twice in the ordinary way with the aid of the translation, every word and idiom being committed to memory together with any peculiarities in grammatical construction.[1] The method of reading should then be reversed, i.e. a sentence or clause of the English translation should be read *first* and then the corresponding sentence or clause of the Urdu. If this is done aloud with the aid of a Munshi, such a revision can be made very rapidly. Difficult paragraphs and phrases should be marked and remarked

[1] To use a singular verb in Hindūstānī after such words as *ṣāḥib*, *munshī*, etc., or after the proper names of respectable people, is as vulgar as to say in English 'you is' or 'these is'.

at each revision. When the student can pick up the English translation and translate readily any of the more difficult portions, so that the difficult phrases closely resemble the original, he may be said to have made a proper use of the text-book. This matter has also been dealt with in the introduction to my *Hindustani Manual*, and attention is directed to the remarks contained in it. One candidate who passed the High Proficiency in Persian, worked in this way without the aid of any Munshi, and the first translation into Persian he ever wrote was in the examination hall. (He of course had also practised talking with Persians or Afghans).

Translating from the English in the manner indicated is one of the best forms of mental gymnastics. The notes and references in this translation have been largely made with the object of inducing the student to use it as a book of exercises for retranslation into Urdu.

If the text-book is mastered in the manner indicated, the candidate will be able to translate with ease into Urdu any English passage set in the examination, as well as the unknown passage of Urdu into English. Further he will have acquired a fund of colloquial knowledge, which however he must practise in conversation, in order to train his tongue as well as his ear.

My thanks are due to Shams-ul-'Ulamā Mawlavī Muḥammad Yūsuf Ja'farī, Khān Bahādur, for valuable help in the preparation of this translation, and also to Babu Nibaran Chandra Chatterji, 2nd Clerk, Board of Examiners, who assisted in the correction of the proofs.

D. C. P.

CALCUTTA:
1910.

TABLE OF CONTENTS.

PART I.

PART II.

The Vazir of Lankuran.

PART III.

Historical Events.

PART I.

1. MOTHERLY AFFECTION.

The mother[1] is seated with her child in her lap. The father is smoking his *ḥuqqa* and is regarding them with happy looks. The child is lying with its eyes open and sucking its thumb. Its mother is regarding it with looks full of affection and is saying lovingly, "My life! When will that day come when thou wilt prattle sweetly? Thou wilt grow up. I shall be old. Thou wilt earn wages and feed thyself and me too." The child smiles and the mother is delighted. When it sticks out its tiny lip and looks as if it were about to cry, the mother gets perturbed. Its swing-cradle is hanging[2] before her. If it has to be lulled to sleep, she places it in it. At night she takes the infant to bed with her. If it wakes up, she starts out of her sleep. If it begins to cry in its first light sleep,[3] the poor mother, overcome by her great maternal affection, will sit up awake, carrying it even up till midnight.[4] In the morning when the child's eyes open, she will sit up. When the sun is up, she washes its face and says to it, "What a pretty moon-like face it has become now! How nice, how nice!"

[1] In the picture. The lithographs of the original are not reproduced. Reference to them is occasionally made in the text.

[2] An Indian cradle is often a swing.

[3] *Kachchī nīṅd*, the half-sleep before going into a sound sleep.

[4] Note force of the repetition in *ādhī ādhī rāt tak*.

2. THE BOY GOING TO SCHOOL.

How quickly he walks so as to arrive in time and not be late. He is thinking to himself[1] that he must repeat[2] properly the

[1] Direct narration.

[2] Note this meaning of *sunānā*. *Sunā,iye* would be impersonal Imperative "one must—."

lesson learnt yesterday, and answer all the questions asked[1] him, and be distinguished amongst the boys. The master too knows him to be anxious to learn.[2] He is first in his class and gets the highest marks in examinations. He treats his master with respect. After work it is good to play, which strengthens the limbs [*lit.* makes the hands and feet active] and refreshes the mind. Certainly he seems to be a promising boy. He will gain knowledge in a short time and be greatly honoured by people, and will acquire wealth and keep alive the name of his ancestors.

[1] Note the method of forming a passive.

[2] *Shauqīn*, adjective, from *shauq* "desire, eagerness, keenness, hobby." *Baṛā shauqīn shikārī hai*, "he is a keen sportsman."

3. THE BOYS ARE PLAYING.[1]

It is necessary to play too during the day to refresh the mind and stretch the limbs and make the body supple. Look, the boys have finished[2] their lessons and have come out of school. They are playing in the play-ground. How happy they are! How free from anxious thought! How fresh and bright are their faces! They are loved by their parents, they are the darlings of their homes. They skip, and jump, and run. Look at this boy: his feet are never on the ground. That boy over there is very active, but this one is ungainly and can't run well—still he runs and gets about. But see he has fallen. What matter? he'll get up again and begin to run. Childhood is a great thing. Well *Miyāṅs*,[3] play, jump, skip, run; but don't think all day of play and play only.[4] Boys, who think of nothing all day but play, look foolish when they

[1] The Present Tense might signify "play habitually." but *khel-rahe haiṅ* means "are playing now"; *vide* Phillott's Hindustani Manual, p. 85 (2).

[2] Note this signification of the Conjunctive Participle.

[3] *Miyāṅ* shows they were Muslim boys.

[4] Note the force of *hī*.

come to repeat their lessons to their master; the master gets angry with them; their parents don't love them: knowledge is great riches; they remain excluded from it.

4. THE CAMEL-SAWĀR.

What a fine female riding-camel! How smoothly it is moving! See how its neck is thrown back! Bravo! it dances along like a peacock. What can one say in praise of the riding-camel? In sandy deserts neither *ekkās* nor carts can travel, and horses and ponies, too, lose heart and lie down for hours without rising. In such places, the camel alone is of use; moreover, it is such a goer that, if it is a good camel, it makes a forced march of as much as fifty *kos*. Where is this camel-rider going? He must have started with [1] something important. Where there are no railways or ḍāks, and where there is sandy desert, and the roads are bad, there, from time immemorial, the camel-sawārs alone transport letters, etc. They carry Mahājans' bills of exchange, thousands of rupees, hundreds of gold mohurs, and very heavy silver and gold jewellery and precious stones, and deliver them in the exact state they receive them. They generally travel by night to escape the glare of the sun; they get through their march during the dark, and while it is still cool they reach the halting-place.

[1] *Le-jātā hogā* "must be carrying" would be better.

5. THE CAMEL BEING LOADED.

Gunny bags, full of grain, are placed on the ground; they will be loaded [1] on the camel. While they load it, the poor beast keeps on opening its mouth wide and crying out. Sometimes it raises its head,[2] and sometimes it bends its neck. Perhaps it is making this complaint, "This cruel camel-man is maltreating me unjustly."

[1] "Which they will load." Note this method of forming the Passive.

[2] *Lit.*, lifts up its neck. Note the Urdu idiom.

Why doesn't it run away? How *can* it escape? One of its knees is tied.

Some camels are not laden. *Kajāwas* are put on them, and people sit comfortably in them on both sides. Whether they lie or go to sleep, the camel goes on. There are female camels, too, in the line, with their young. The young one follows close [1] behind its mother, while she keeps on looking back and continually regarding it with looks of affection: if it lags the least behind, she gets perturbed. What can she do? She is helpless and can't stand still, for her nose-string [2] is tied to the camel in front of her. The camel is very useful in sandy countries. In the first place, it can travel easily in sand; and in the second,[3] there is a scarcity of water in those parts and it is this poor beast alone that can do without water —for several days even.

[1] Similarly *āge jā,o* is "go on ahead," but *āge āge jā,o* is "keep just in front of me."

[2] *Nakel* is, I think, the short nose-string and perhaps includes the nose-peg. *Mahār* is, I think, the long rope. *Shutur be-mahār*, met., means, "refractory, uncontrolled."

[3] *Ek to—— ——dusre————*.

6. THE PAṆḌIT JĪ'S BULLOCK CART.

How light it is! How handsome it is in shape! It is nicely painted too. It is the work of a skilled workman. The bedding is white [*i.e.*, not coloured]; the curtains are white. On one side the Paṇḍit has let down the curtain to ward off the sun; on the other side he has turned it up (on the roof) to let in the breeze. The bullocks, too, are fine and appear to be from Nagor.[1]

The Great [2] Paṇḍit Jī is sitting in the cart. See how the dog has bounded forward and is barking at the bullocks, which, however, stand still without any concern. Formerly the

[1] Nagor, in Gujerat, is famous for its bullocks.

[2] Pandits, etc., are addressed as Mahārāj.

wealthy of this country used to drive about in *raths*,[1] but other people used *bahlīs*.[1] These are vehicles of olden times. They progress slowly and are jolty. Since baggīs and railways were introduced, they have become less valued. Baniyas and Mahājans [2] still use them, and they enter too into marriage processions.[3]

[1] *Rath*, m., a large two-wheeled bullock carriage; *also* a war-chariot drawn by horses.

Bahlī, f., is a small bullock carriage.

[2] *Mahājan*, a Hindu banker.

[3] *Barāt*, f., the marriage procession when the bridegroom goes to the bride's house for the marriage ceremony.

7. DRIVING IN A *EKKĀ*.

The *ekkā* has started from the sarāy. One man has taken his seat; another has come, one bundle in his oxter and another in his hand. The *ekkāwālā* has stopped his pony[1]; he will take him up and then start off. If he comes across one or two more passengers on the road, he will take them up too.

"Mr. Ekkā-wālā, what's in this bag?"

"My *ḥuqqa* and *chilam*."[2]

"Where do you put your passengers' shoes?"

"I put them too in the bag."

"Where will you take your passengers?"[3]

"To Mian Mir."

"How far is that?"

"Four *kos*."

"What do you charge for one seat?"

"One *ānā*."

"How much do you earn in one day?"

"Ten or twelve *ānās*."

"What does the horse's up-keep cost you?"

[1] *Ghorā*, a general term, includes pony.

[2] *Ḥuqqa* is the water-bowl and *chilam* is the earthenware top.

[3] *Sawārī*, "a conveyance, a passenger; *also* riding or driving."

"Five or six *ānās* a day, that is, two or two-and-a-half *ānās* for grass, two *ānās* for gram,[1] and one-and-a-half or two[2] for *nihārī*."[3]

"How much did you pay for the pony?"

"Forty rupees."

"How does it go?"

"It goes pretty well. On a *pakkā* road, it takes us to our destination by noon."

"Why have you tied bells on its neck?"

"For ornament; besides they sound nice."

"Which is most used in the Panjab, *ekkās* or *bahlīs*?"

"*Ekkās*. For poor people, Ṣāḥib, this sort of conveyance is good enough, but it is certainly very shaky and jolty."

1 *Dāna*, properly "grain," is vulgarly gram. *Ekkāwālās* always feed on gram.

2 Note order *do derh*, not *derh do* as in English.

3 *Nihārī* is the pick-me-up given to horses and ponies on a journey. An ordinary receipt is 2 oz. of turmeric, up to 1 lb. of *guṛ*, and an equal quantity of *āṭā*. *Nihārī* also means the morning feed.

8. THE RĀJĀ ṢĀḤIB'S ELEPHANT.

Listen a bit! I hear the sound of bells. Perhaps an elephant is coming this way—come let's go and (enjoy a) look at it. Oh see! there it is. How it swings along towards us! Oh, oh! what a big elephant! What long tusks it's got, and how handsome they look with their brass binding. There is a plume on its head. Large bells are slung on both of its sides, and it was these that made the clanging sound we heard. There is a silver *hauda* on its back, in which the Rājā Ṣāḥib always sits.[1] But it's very high! How can he get up into it? A ladder always[2] hangs at the side and the *mahāwat* makes the elephant sit down. The elephant is very obedient to its

1 *Baiṭhte hain*, Present Tense, "sits habitually"; but *baiṭhe* (*hū, e*) *hain* "is seated, is sitting."

2 *Laṭaktā rahnā.*

mahāwat's commands, so much so that it works at a mere sign, *i.e.*, it gets up, sits down, moves on and stands still.

When the mahāwat orders it, it raises its trunk to its forehead and salutes the Rājā Ṣāḥib.

9. THE BAGGĪ[1]-HORSE.

This horse is being trained to go in harness [*lit.* for a *baggī*]. When it goes well, it will be harnessed in the *baggī*. The coachman first took[2] it into an open piece of ground and tied a longish bit of rope to its bridle and lunged it well. It is now quiet and subdued and will be put in a *ghasīṭā.*[3] When the horse was harnessed the first time, it plunged a great deal and was alarmed and said to itself, " What the devil is this on my neck ? " But the coachman knows his business. By patting, and 'tongueing' to it, and making much of it, and coaxing it, he has quieted it [*lit.* made it straight]; and its wildness and fright have disappeared. Look, it is now working pretty well; it turns by a mere 'feeling' of the reins. How well it lifts its feet! How well it trots! Of course, when it misbehaves, it is whipped for it. A clever teacher, too, when he sets young pupils to work, treats them at first just like this, with kindness [*lit.* affection] and gentleness. For a few days he explains things encouragingly, and then by degrees the child improves. It is only this way good boys learn to read and write,[4] but those who shirk get punished.

1 *Baggī*, a two-wheeled light trap with a hood.

2 Note Pluperfect Tense *le-giyā thā* to indicate a time anterior to the Preterite.

3 *Ghasīṭā*, a rough wooden frame without wheels, for breaking in horses; from the verb *ghasīṭnā*, to drag along the ground.

4 Note the Hindustani idiom is "to write and read."

10. TENT-PEGGING.

What is going on here ? Why is there such a crowd ? Ah, these are preparations for tent-pegging; for this reason the people are drawn up in line. Come, let us look on. Chum, keep back in the line, otherwise you may get in the way of the horses. Look, there is a sawār galloping towards us. How he has let his horse go.[1] He is a good rider too. How tight and close he sits without moving in the saddle. What's more[2] the horse is fast. It comes just like an arrow. Look! it's now close to the peg. It looks as though its belly touched the ground. The rider will now take good aim at the peg and carry it off clean, and everybody will cheer him. In front of the carriage there is a Ṣāḥib on foot, in uniform. He is an officer of the *Risāla*, and has a book in his hand, in which he is writing the names. Prizes will be given to the winners. Tent-pegging is a military accomplishment, combining play and exercise as well. This practice is often carried out by Native Cavalry Regiments; and why not, for by such things the activity and alertness of the sepoys is increased, and these qualities prove useful in the time of need.

[1] *Sarpaṭ dauṛānā*, tr., is "to go at full gallop." [2] *Ghoṛā bhī—*.

11. CROSSING IN A FERRY BOAT.

To-day the river is in flood; there has been very heavy rain somewhere. How broad the river has become! People cannot now cross to this side without a boat, nor go to that. See, the boat has left our bank. The boatmen are propelling the boat with poles. How crammed the boat is!

The boat has now reached mid-stream. Look, the boatmen have suddenly begun to yell. What has happened? The boat is not sinking I hope? No: when the boat reaches mid-stream, the force of the current is felt, and the boatmen exert their strength and make a clamor, and the passengers, too, join in shouting. Look, the boat has now got beyond the deep water and will soon reach the bank. The passengers will again get flurried and excited, each one trying to disembark first. But haste is a mistake. Be the first to embark, but the last to disembark.

12. THE SWIMMERS IN THE RIVER.

Come let us walk by the river. Hallo![1] how it has risen! Some one has inflated a *mashk* and put it under his chest, and is floating down-stream on the tide; but only a man, who has no need of such aids and swims by his hands and feet alone, is to be counted a real swimmer. Swimming is a useful accomplishment. If a swimmer can't get a (ferry) boat, he just makes a few strokes and is on the other side. Should a boat sink, it is a terrible calamity for all. Those, who can't swim, lose their lives, but swimmers by swimming save themselves as well as one or two others besides. This, too, is a kind of athletic exercise, and aids digestion, and reduces fat. Come, let us, too, both have a swim and see who can swim the farthest. Chum![2] it is better to keep near the ghāṭ.[3] There's no good in turning oneself into a fish and lying for hours in the water, losing one's wind, and getting ducked or being drowned in a whirlpool.

[1] *Oho*, exclamation of surprise.

[2] *Bhā,ī*; not a term of great affection; it is polite and can be applied even to servants, but not to superiors.

[3] *Ghāṭ*, "a bathing place with steps; a place to draw water; a ferry."

13. WRESTLERS AND WRESTLING.

The spectators are collected round about the arena. A pair of Indian clubs is placed in readiness. These two gymnasts have gone down[1] into the arena and thrown off their clothes, and tightened their loin-cloths. What make and shape! They look as if they had been cast in a mould. What bodies they have! Smooth and shining[2] like glass. Gymnastic exercises are a fine thing; they keep a man healthy, and his body gradually becomes finely developed; appetite is promoted; anything eaten is easily digested; the limbs are made active so

[1] Lower than the surrounding platform.

[2] Wrestlers train on *ghī*, which perhaps accounts for the expression.

that one cannot help longing to exercise one's strength. Look; they slap their biceps and face each other. There; they've shaken hands. At one moment, one pushes the other and drives him back; at another, the other drives him with his head. Each is intent on getting an opportunity to practise a wrestling trick and throw his adversary flat on his back. If the wrestling has been fair and there has been no dispute, people will clap. The *Miyāṅ* [a Muslim term in address] that throws the other will swagger, unable to contain himself through pride; but the one who is thrown will hang his head from shame.

14. THE SAWYERS SAWING WOOD.

What hard wood it is! The saw makes slow way through it, and the sawdust produced too is little.

"Oh sawyers! What wood is this?"

"It's *sāl*,[1] *Ṣāḥib*. Since this morning up till now we have been able to saw only four or five[2] planks, and our arms are quite tired."

"To what uses is this kind of wood put?"

"As a rule planks, beams, and chairs are made of it."

"What other different kinds of wood are found here?"

"*Shīsham*[3]—*diyār*.[4] Of these *shīsham* is the strongest and most expensive. Chairs, small chests, and small wooden boxes are generally made from it; but it is not sufficiently abundant for boards and beams to be made of it. In the Panjab, *diyār*[4] wood is generally used. Weevils don't attack it, and it is cheap. Hence it is much used for building purposes, and in railway workshops. Quantities of chests, almiras,[5] and tables, are made of it. Ṣāḥib, the fact is, in this world, wood is a very useful thing, and we, especially, earn our living by it."

[1] *Sāl*, the teak tree.

[2] *Pāṅch chār*, generally *chār pāṅch*.

[3] *Shīsham*, the sisso, *Dalbergia sissoo*.

[4] *Diyār*, the deodar; the Himalayan Cedar.

[5] *Almārī*, (from Port. almario), "a wardrobe; a press; a book-case."

15. THE *DARZĪ* SEWING CLOTHES.

This is a clever workman. He cuts and fits the figure[1] well, and there is no bagging left anywhere. He sews well too. His double hem-stitch is very fine. Another good point about him is that even if a very small bit of your cloth remains over, he gives it back to you; and for these qualities he is famous. A heap of clothes to be made, is always [2] lying in his shop. His work cannot be finished by himself alone: he has [3] apprentices. He sews himself, and makes them work too, and gives out work to poor women as well. "Well, Mr. Darzī, you make good clothes certainly, but you take a long time; you promise to deliver in two days but take eight."

"Ṣāḥib, what can I do? I have much work and only a few workers. I do my very best but still I fall behindhand."

1 *Lit.* "he cuts clothes so well that they——."

2 *Lagā-rahnā*, to remain always.

3 *Biṭhā-rakhnā*; "has sat them down and kept them"; force of both verbs.

16. THE FISHERMEN NETTING.

There is a net spread in the river, and three men are dragging it. It seems that a lot of fish have come into it. See; how dear life is to them! How bewildered they are; they seek a means of escape; they leap, they jump; they are enmeshed in the net, but what can they do? A net is not a thing from which escape is possible. They will now be taken out of the net, and carried to market, and hawked about the streets.

Are there any other methods of catching fish?

Yes, many. There are several kinds of nets. In shallow water, big baskets are used. Some sportsmen [*lit.* keen people] catch fish with rods.

"What's that [a rod]?"

It's a thin stick of bamboo, thick at one end and thin at the other. One end of a line is fastened to the thin end of the bamboo, and at the other end of the line there is a hook.

The fishermen, when fishing, bait the hook with a pill of *āṭā*, or a very small bit of meat. The hook pierces the fish's throat, and the poor thing becomes powerless and falls into the power of the fisherman.

17. THE HORSE BEING SHOD.

One sāis is standing there holding the leading rope. The farrier is paring the hoof. A boy has drawn near and begun to look on. He has never seen a horse shod. Wonderingly he asks what they [1] are doing, and why they are cutting its feet.

The farrier replies: "*Miyāṅ*, we're not cutting its feet, we're paring its hoofs. We'll put on [implant] shoes. These are a great protection; gravel and stones won't hurt [pierce] its feet; the horse feels comfortable and can work hard."

"Well, just tell me, isn't paring the hoofs painful?"

"*Miyāṅ*, only when one pares the quick. We pare the hard part of the hoof, just as the barber [2] pares your nails."

"*Oho*! [3] what long nails you are driving in. Won't they draw blood?"

"*Miyāṅ*, they're driven into the hard part of the hoof. If driven into the soft part, they would draw blood."

"This horse is standing quietly on three legs. Why doesn't it free its leg?"

"It's a quiet horse. Had there been a vicious horse, you would have seen how it would have jumped about and let fly with its heels, and been managed with great difficulty."

[1] Direct narration. "Asks that 'What are you doing?'" For form *kāṭe-ḍālnā* 'vide' *Hind. Stumbling-Blocks.*

[2] *Nā,ī.* An Indian barber cuts hair, nails, and corns; and also cleans the ears and circumcises.

[3] For surprise.

18. THE BANIYĀ'S SHOP.

The Baniyā, scales in hand, is weighing out his wares; his customers are standing in front of him. What a large shop it is! Every kind of thing is exposed for sale, and whatever is there, is good of its kind. How piled up high are the baskets of *dāl*, rice, and *āṭā!* Come, let us purchase at this shop.

"*Lālā Jī!* Give me two rupees' worth of *ghī* and one rupee's worth of *āṭā*."

"Here it is [*lit.* Please take]."

"At what rate will you sell?"

"*Ghī*, one and a quarter seer the rupee; *āṭā* fifteen seers."

"Give me somewhat more than this."

"I'm not overcharging [1]; ask where you like."

"All right; weigh."

This is a very smart shopman. No matter how great the crowd of buyers, he never loses his head in the least; he serves everybody in a moment. Don't judge him by his dirty, soiled clothes; he's a wealthy man; he buys thousands of rupees worth of grain every year. Should a small army encamp here, he can, unaided, supply rations for it. He has many large houses (mansions) of his own, and shops let to others.

[1] *Lit.* "there is no difference (between my charge and the *nirḵh*)."

19. THE DHOBI WASHING.

He works hard. In the evening he boils the clothes. In the morning, he loads his bullock and takes the load to the *ghāṭ*. Sometimes he works in the *nālā*, sometimes in the river. If it is the cold weather, he suffers from the cold; and if it is the hot season, the sun [*lit.* sunshine] scorches him. See, it is near noon and he is still standing in the water and sorting the clothes. See his wife [the *dhobin*] has brought his dinner. His small son is fond of play and forgets to feel hungry; he is busy flying his kite.

"Well, Mr. Dhobī, where is your home?"

"Ṣāḥib, that village in front of you—there I live."

"Is that your bullock?"

"Yes."

"How much did you pay for it?"

"Fifteen rupees."

"See—the dog is lying there watching (your dinner)."

"Ṣāḥib—he's not a pilferer; he's my *chaukī-dār*. Please see; the gentlemen's clothes are spread out to dry on the ground; dare anyone come near them?"

"*Dhobī*, your profession is a good one. You cleanse clothes from dirt and give people clean clothes to wear [1]."

[1] Note the use of the causal.

20. TAKING THE AIR IN THE MORNING.

It is morning. One feels cheerful. Come, let us go for a little walk into the garden and take the air. Āhā! [1] What a very nice cool breeze there is! There are [2] all sorts of flowers here. I was delighted the moment I entered. Just [3] look at the green; how refreshing (or resting) it is to the sight! Green grass you call it? [4] Rather it's [5] a carpet of green velvet. The drops of dew on it have the appearance of embedded pearls. The beauty and delight of the trees is peculiar to themselves; some are laden with flowers, others with fruit. The branches are waving; the well is working.

"What is this *mālī* doing?"

"He is planting out young plants."

"Come let us watch him."

"Ancient man, whence have you brought these plants?"

"Young Sir, from the *Pādshāhī Bāgh*."

"In how many days will these seeds germinate?"

"They will sprout quickly."

"What's in the *ghaṛā* [earthen pot, globular and porous]?"

"Water."

"What for?"

[1] *Āhā* for admiration.

[2] Note the verb in the Hindustani idiom.

[3] *Ẓarā*.

[4] Note the idiom.

[5] Note the verb in the Hindustani idiom; [not "is"].

"I'll water the plants with it, and they will then soon revive."

21. THE CAMEL.

"Come, let me show you a picture. Tell me all[1] the things you see in it [*lit.* tell me 'What various things do you see in it?']."

"There is a *siris*[2] tree, called in the Panjab *sirīn*. At the foot of the tree, a camel-man is sitting.[3] A *ḥuqqa* is in front of him. There is another camel-man standing up, but his back is towards us."

"How many camels are there?"

"Seven. One is lying down with its tail [back] turned towards us, and one has a rope tied to its muzzle; one has broken a branch, and is eating the leaves, and, behind the camel-man, one camel is standing up, and one is lying down. On the right, one has lowered its head and is eating grass; and near it, one is lying down, where the two small trees are. On one side [of the picture], too, the loads of the camels are lying."

Did you notice the shape of the camel? Of what a strange fashion it is! A smallish head, long and thin legs and neck, the back high in the middle. Hence the common saying, "Oh camel, oh! what part[4] of you is straight?" But if you consider well (you will see) that no point is without some benefit to the camel. See, if its neck[5] were not long, how could it graze[5] on the ground? How could it drink[5] water? If its legs were short, how could it eat the leaves of trees? A horse is restrained by the bridle, but the camel by the *nakel*. See, a very small rope is in its nose and (yet) such a great animal as

[1] *Kyā kyā* and direct narration.

[2] *Siris*, the siris tree, *Albizzia Lebbek* or *Acacia Sirissa.*

[3] "Is seated."

[4] *Kal* is generally machinery, or a piece of a machine.

[5] "Had not been long"; "could have grazed"; "could have drunk": Past Conditional Tenses.

this is powerless. In reality it belongs to [1] countries where sand abounds, and water is scarce. For this reason, God has made its body suitable to the country. See, its eye-lids are thick and hanging down, and are a great protection to its eyes.

In the hot season,[2] the glare is intense in the desert and these eye-lids protect the poor thing's eyes from the heat and glare. The nostrils are so constructed that it can close them at will, and this is a great comfort to it; for in the desert violent dust-storms arise and sand in whole heaps is lifted up and carried along to another place. Then this poor thing closes its nostrils and is saved from the discomfort of the sand. It has two [3] long lips, so strong that it can break off the twigs of bushes with them. The upper lip is divided; if it has to catch hold of anything, it can do so by means of it. God has so constructed its mouth that the thorns of the bushes (it feeds on) do not pierce it at all. The camel is partial to thorny bushes [*lit.* thorny bushes are very pleasing [4] to it], and these are generally found in the desert. Grass, the leaves of trees, whether bitter or astringent, in short whatever it meets with, is its fodder. God has given it such a stomach that if it drinks large quantities of water at a time, it is sufficient for it for five or six days.

On its back is a shapeless heap of fat called the hump, and the strange thing about it is that if [5] the camel gets nothing to eat for several [6] days at a time, this fat dissolves and forms its nutriment. If you look attentively, you will perceive that there are two toes on its feet [7] furnished with nails. The feet are broad and soft and springy underneath, like the cushions of a *baggī* (carriage). This is the reason that they grip [7] the sand

1 "——to *those* countries where ———": note the Urdu idiom for future translation.

2 Note the plural.

3 *Lambe lambe.—Vide* '*Hindustani Stumbling-Blocks.*'

4 *Bhānā*, intr.

5 *Jab*, "when."

6 *Ka,ī ka,ī.*

7 In the original the singular is used.

(without slipping), but in mud they [1] slip, and the poor beast has a bad fall.

When they wish [2] to load the camel, they seize the *nakel* and make it squat. The poor beast keeps on opening its mouth and making a noise; it shakes its head, but it is loaded just the same.

When there were no *ḍāks* nor railways, it was put to many useful purposes. Still, too, where there are no railways, hundreds of maunds of stuff are transported on camels to various countries. If hills or forests lie in their way, they are not stopped by them.

The riding-camel is faster and handsomer than the baggage camel. The riding camel, male or female, is called a *sāṅḍnī*.[3] It is no great task for it to travel fifty or sixty *kos*.

Camel's milk is drunk (by people), but is not very nice. In some places butter and *ghī* are made from it.[4] From the hair, 'dressing-gowns' and blankets are made.

1 In the original the singular is used.

2 Note, simple Present Tense.

3 Is this correct? I think the female only is called *sāṅḍnī*.

4 In some frontier stations the milk of cows, camels, goats, sheep, etc., eked out by camel-women's milk, is mixed together and sold to the unwary.

22. THE HORSE.

"What people are these in the picture?"

"They are dwellers of Arabia."

"How do [1] you know that?"

"By their dress."

"Tell me all the things there are in the picture."

"There are four date-trees; two are near the tent and two behind the horse but in the distance, and hence they appear small. A very large [2] tent is pitched, the top of which is seen

1 Note the Preterite Tense. The Present Tense would signify "How are you knowing it now?"

2 *Vide* "Hindustani Manual," p. 99 (c), and "Hindustani Stumbling-Blocks."

under the date-trees. In front of it, there is a colt standing and looking round. Near the hind-leg of the colt a saddle is lying and a woman is seated supporting a child. The child is giving the mare grain in his skirt, while the father, spear in hand, is standing by looking on."

Arab horses are noted for their beauty, but the best thing about them is their hardiness in enduring hunger and thirst. In hot weather or cold, they make long stages and do not knock up. In the wilderness, the people of Arabia pitch their tents and live in them. Their tents are their houses, and in them they keep their horses. They treat them as children, and the horses too live like children. The children fondle them and play with them and they play with the children, and never offer them any injury [*lit.* what power have they that—— ?].

The horse is an intelligent beast. It recognises its own stall, knows its master, and what's more it never forgets a road it has traversed once or twice.

There was a mare in a certain village and she was in the habit [1] of going out to graze with her foal. One day she came back to her master's house at a gallop and began to neigh, and it was evident she was distressed. Her master understood that some misfortune [2] or other had happened to her. The mare galloped off neighing, and her master followed close [3] behind. There was a *nālā* near. When she came to it, it was discovered that her foal had fallen into it and could not get out. The master summoned some men and had the foal taken out, and petted the mare very much.

The good point about the horse is that you can train it to do what you like. Cavalry and Artillery horses understand the bugle calls as well as the men do. If men ever fall off their horses on parade, their riderless horses go on with the movements just

1 For this use of *karnā* ' vide ' "*Hindustani Manual*," p. 71 (*a*).

2 *Ṣadma*, " a shock, a blow, an accident, injury, etc."

3 *Pīchhe pīchhe*.

the same.[1] At the sound of the bugle they turn right and left and advance and retire.

When the regiment returns to its lines, they come with it and take their place in their stalls.

It is stated that in a battle a bugler fell off his horse, which somehow or other happened to join the enemy's force. There some other *sipāhī* caught it, and mounted it, and came into the field to fight. The bugler recognised his horse from a distance and sounded a summons on his bugle. As soon as the horse heard it, it ran to the call, and bearing its rider with it, rejoined its own force.

In a battery, once a certain two horses were always harnessed together as a pair. One day the battery was sent on service and one of the horses was killed, but the other returned safe. When it was tied up in its stall, being alone, it began to look all around as though searching for somebody. This horse used always to eat its grain in company with its pair. When its grain was placed before it, it never even touched it. Another horse was brought and placed beside it, but still it wouldn't eat. It remained thus hungry and thirsty. The result was that it died after three days.

However tired and wearied a horse may be, it won't shirk if ridden, or lose heart in the intense heat. Somehow or other it will carry its rider to the journey's end. It often happens that a rider[2] has galloped off and escaped, and this faithful beast has borne him safe to his destination, while it, on arriving, has dropped down dead. Such a thing has only happened when the rider's life has been in danger, for (otherwise) who would be so pitiless as to go overwork a dumb animal?

[1] *Usī ṭaraḥ.* [2] "To riders."

23. THE ELEPHANT.

Several people are going along the road. On the head of one of the women there is a large basket. The elephant has lifted its trunk and is squirting water.

The *darzī* [in the picture] is seated at work in the balcony and the water is falling on his face. The poor fellow has put both his hands in front of his face, but how can they keep off the water? The poor chap is soaked. He was cutting something with his scissors, but they have slipped from his grasp.

Come, let me tell you[1] the story about this elephant and the *darzī*.

It is related that a rich man had a favourite elephant which the *mahāwat* used to take every day to bathe in the river. There was a *darzī's* shop on the road One day the elephant put its trunk into the shop. The *darzī* was eating *chapātīs*, and he put one into the elephant's trunk. The elephant took the *chapātī* and went off. When it came back there next day, it again extended its trunk. The *darzī* too remembered. He had put by some *chapātī* for it, and he gave it that. In this way a friendship sprang up between the two. When the elephant used to come and put its trunk into the shop, the *darzī* used to give it a *chapātī*, or some vegetable, or some fruit. The elephant used to take it, well pleased, and go away. One day the *darzī* was in a bad temper. The elephant came and put in its trunk. The *darzī* pricked it with his needle. The elephant quickly withdrew its trunk and silently went its way. When it was returning from the river, it filled its trunk with a lot of muddy water. When it came near the shop, it lifted its trunk and cast the lot over the *darzī*. The *darzī* was covered with mud. Many good clothes were being made.[2] They too were all spoiled. The elephant went swinging away,[3] while the *darzī* remained behind looking foolish.

Look at God's power;[4] what a great shape! What an ungainly form it has; still it is not at all deficient in activity. It can understand, too, a mere sign, just like a man. Its

1 *Sunānā*, "to cause to hear."

2 "Sewed"; *vide* Hindustani Manual, p. 157 (*d*).

3 Meaningless appositive; *vide* Hindustani Manual, p. 170 (*c*).

4 *Qudrat* also means Nature.

courage is such that it fights the tiger. When it trumpets, the tiger's heart throbs with fear. Look at its head; it looks like two water-melons joined together. It has two small eyes. Its power of sight is not great, but its hearing is acute. From a distance if it discerns a foot-fall, it at once becomes alert.

Its tusks are long and handsome. Once a year—sometimes every third or fourth year—they are cut, but grow out again. You must have seen [1] the things that are manufactured from ivory. How handsome they are! Most males have tusks like these (in the picture). Besides these tusks, the elephant has other teeth in its head, by means of which it eats its food. Hence the common proverb: 'The elephant has one set of teeth for eating, another for show.' This proverb is cited when a man has one thing in his heart and another on his tongue. Look at its trunk; how long it is: this is its nose, and this too is a hand to it. By it, it lifts up everything, and by its means, it eats its fodder. In it, it can suck up a whole *mashk* full of water, and by it, it discharges the water into its mouth and drinks. By it, it seizes small branches of trees and fans itself. On the end [2] of the trunk there is a quite small thing which serves it as a finger. When it (the elephant) lies down in its stall, it first spreads grass or branches of trees for itself.[3] If it turns over to another side, it puts the bedding on the other side. The elephant delights in water. It dives into the river and sticks the end of its trunk out of the water and remains under for hours. When the elephant is standing in its stall, it throws up earth on to its head in play, but when being ridden it never scatters the dust like this. It can be taught to do many things [*lit.* by teaching it learns a great deal]. For every action there are special words. At special sounds, it eats, drinks, lies down, gets up, stands still, picks up any fallen object that the *mahāwat* may indicate, and salams.

1 *Maiṅ ne dekhā hogā* "I must have seen."

2 *Sirā.*

3 ——— *lenā*; 'vide' *Hindustani Manual*, p. 80 (c).

When the *mahāwats* give[1] it the daily allowance of food,[2] they make the food into very big mouthfuls, and wrapping them round in grass, keep on placing them in the trunk. If the *mahāwat* is a pilferer,[3] he points out a mouthful and the elephant keeps it concealed in its throat, and when the *mahāwat* comes alone and asks for it, then it takes it out and returns it to him exactly as it was. See what a large animal it is, and yet there is no necessity for a *nakel*, nor need for a bridle. The *mahāwat* sits upon the elephant's neck and guides it by his feet only.

The elephant is ridden by kings and by rich people. Those who go out tiger-shooting ride elephants and shoot the tigers with rifles. Elephants transport[4] many heavy things for buildings and bear them across rivers and *nālās*. They drag great guns and transport the baggage of troops. Before the introduction of artillery, they were of great use in war; but, in the first place, this animal is terrified of fire, and, in the second place, if struck by a round shot, the poor beast drops as though it were a house falling; and also if it flees in terror from the roar of artillery, it tramples under foot men of its own force, in its flight. For this reason elephants are not now used[5] in war.

There is no elephant forest in the Panjab; but there are many in[6] Bengal, Behar, and in the Dakan. Elephants generally live in forests where there are dense trees. In such forests whole herds wander about. In each herd, there are only the elephants of one family. Sometimes families mix, but if there is an alarm, then each family forms a separate band. The elephants wander far and wide in the jungle, but they always move as a well-organized body. One goes ahead to act as a scout, and this is generally an old female. When they sleep, one or other of them keeps alert and acts as a *chaukīdār*. This too is generally a female.

1 "Feed it." 2 *Rātib.* 3 *Choṭṭā*, a petty thief.

4 *Ḍhonā*, to carry, especially on the head or shoulder, as *qulīs* do *Ḍhonā*, to wash.

5 'Vide' *Hind. Man.*, p. 164 (*b*). 6 *Kī ṭaraf*, or *meṅ*.

If a herd has to be captured, the following plan is adopted:—Many men join and go into the part of the forest where elephants live, and when they learn that the elephants are in a certain spot, they surround them, and in two or three hours enclose them in a circle of bamboo fencing. This circle is six or seven miles in circumference. Inside this circle, is made a second, and smallish, circle of poles.[1] This is made under cover of dense trees and in a[2] spot where elephants come and go. They make a door in it four yards wide. Leading up to the door from a distance of fifty yards, they make something like a double '*machān*' (pāṛ), and, on the inner side of the *machān*, they dig a ditch. When they have finished doing this, they fire off guns and make a noise. When the elephants come into the circle, they at once close the door.

There are several means of catching a single solitary elephant, one of which is the following, but it is one with great risk to life. They take three or four trained elephants with very thick and strong ropes. One end[3] of the rope is tied to the (each) elephant, and at the other end is a noose. Three men ride each elephant—the *mahāwat* on the neck, the noose-thrower on the back, the *relne-wālā*[4] on the quarters near the tail. When the wild elephant comes near, they chase it on the elephants and when they get within casting-distance,[5] the noosers from here and there cast the nooses on the neck of the wild elephant and snare the poor thing.

When a young one is born, the whole herd remains on the spot for two or three days with the mother. During this time the young one begins to run about and becomes fit for a journey. If it is necessary to cross a river, the mother stays behind its young one which it keeps in front of her, supporting

[1] The description is by no means clear.
[2] "In *such* a spot that ——."
[3] *Sirā.*
[4] I do not know what *relne-wālā* "butter, or shover" means here.
[5] *Zad*, f., is the Persian for *mār*, f., H., "striking-distance." *Shahr qil'a kī mār* (or *zad*) *ke andar hai*=" the fort commands the city."

it with her trunk. When it is three or four months old, it swims unaided or else mounts [1] on its mother's shoulders.

The elephant attains maturity in twenty-five years, and in thirty-five years becomes very strong; and it generally attains this age. Some live to a hundred or even more.

[1] Note the force of *lenā* in *chaṛh-letā hai*.

24. THE BUFFALO.[1]

See, there are several buffalos in the tank The back, horns, and part of the head of one are visible; the rest of the body is in the water: of one only, the head appears. The herdsman is standing on the land with a stick [2] in his hand and throwing bricks at one to get it out of the water.

The buffalo [1] is a very ungainly and awkward animal and can't run [from fear] for even a short distance. Boys drive whole herds and take them to the jungle; they mount [3] on their backs and ride them, and as soon as it is evening they bring them all home again.

The buffalo feels the heat very much. It delights in mud or water. If it comes across any water, whether canal or tank, it immediately rushes into it. If the water is deep, it stands up in it; if shallow, it immediately lies down and hides its whole body with the exception of its muzzle, which it sticks out of the water so as to be able to breathe, and it is for this reason that God has given it a long neck compared with the cow.

The buffalo is a very powerful beast. If it is necessary to cross a stream with a strong current, they [4] drive the buffalos

[1] Note that *bhaiṅs* the generic word is feminine. *Bhaiṅsā* is a bull-buffalo.

[2] *Liye* the participle (inflected as the verb is transitive, 'vide' *Hindustani Stumbling-Blocks*) indicates state, and signifies that the stick was in his hand before he came on the scene.

[3] *Chaṛh-baiṭhnā*; meaning of both verbs retained, *vide* Hindustani Manual, p. 80 (*b*) (2).

[4] People, *i.e.*, the villagers or herdsmen: note this colloquialism.

into the stream and hold on to their tails and cross to the other side. The buffalo cares nothing for the force of the current. If the water is deep, it swims. If the herdsman is not a swimmer, he mounts the buffalo, but the danger is that whenever the buffalo likes it lies down and the helpless rider is left to himself.

The buffalo gives much more milk than the cow, and the milk too is thicker and yields more butter; but the flavour of cow's milk is better.

Bull-buffalos are used as beasts of burden, and carry a greater load than bullocks. They convey thousands of maunds of grain and other things, from town to town.

Even crows think this quiet animal sluggish. They come and settle on it and peck it, but the buffalo benefits by this; for there are bots [*lit.* insects] in the buffalos' bodies and the crows pick these out. When the buffalo is milked, its calf is placed near it; for until the calf has tried to suck a little, no milk will descend from the udder. This is a good thing for the owner, for the calf is kept tied up at home and the mother sent out to graze, and so the cowherd can't milk the buffalo. This peculiarity is not found in the goat. Whoever he may be, he can milk one whenever he likes.

As much as the tame buffalo is quiet, the wild one is vicious. The wild male is called *arnā bhaiṅsā*.[1] It is so powerful that if it charges and butts, it can knock down even an elephant.

[1] Also *arnā*, alone.

25. THE COW.

This animal is too well known to need description. The Hindus consider it to be a very holy animal; they consider it not merely an animal but something much more. This is the reason that they cherish it so much and take such care of it. Perhaps no animal is so beneficial to man as the cow. While it lives, it yields us many things for eating and drinking. It is obligatory on us, in return, to care well for an animal that renders us so many benefits. First of all it gives us milk, sweet and fresh. What boy or girl is there that will not wish to drink a cup when one is before him? Cream, curds, butter, *ghī*, are obtained from the cow. If these things were not to be had, how tasteless our food and drink would be. Bullocks plough the land (*zamīn par*), carry loads, draw carts, and work wells and oil-presses. Mud houses (*kachche makān*) are smeared with cow-dung, and cakes for burning too are made from it,[1] and poor people who cannot afford (——*kā maqdūr na-honā*) to burn wood, burn these Many parts of the cow's body are of use after it dies. From the hide are made, harness for horses, necessary furniture for *baggīs*, saddles, whips, bridles, and many other things: from its horns, combs, handles for penknives and dinner-knives, etc.; and from its sinews, etc., glue.

The cow is milked twice daily, morning and evening. The milk is boiled in earthen vessels and set aside, and is then used for any purpose that may be desired. If butter has to be made, a very small quantity of *dahī* (sour curds) is added to the milk, which is then covered: it curdles and becomes *dahī*. The *dahī* is then put into an earthen vessel and made into butter. In some countries butter is made (*makkhan nikālnā*) in various other ways, but everywhere by shaking.

The cow generally eats grass. Grain and oil-cake (*khalī*) are also given to it to increase the yield of milk. It does not eat meat nor any living thing.[2] Every one is familiar with its shape and make, but many people do not know that animals that chew the cud have a peculiar form of stomach (*mi'da*).[3]

[1] *Uplā* is the dung cake, and *thāpnā* is making it by patting.

[2] In the Persian Gulf, locusts, fish, and dates are given to horses and cows. Indian cows eat dry bones if found in the jungle. Buffalos will eat litter and dung freely, and *gwālās* will buy up litter from stables in quantities, as fodder.

[3] Not *peṭ* here. *Mi'da* means the inside of the stomach only.

26. THE ASS.

See this unsympathetic (*be-dard*) man, how mercilessly he beats his donkey. The poor beast is so overladen that it stumbles as it comes along. What! is not this a creature of God? The *Miyāṅ* will only then understand the true state of things when he bears the load on his own back.

Admitted that the donkey is not beautiful. Certainly its ears are long, and from its general appearance it seems moribund. It suffers from men's tyrannies, and it is *these* that have abased it. Still God has not created it devoid of understanding. On several occasions (*maqām*), it has shown great intelligence. If its master is kind to it, it too will love him in return. It lifts its feet somewhat slowly, still in spite of that (*magar is par bhī*) it travels on for hours at a stretch. On bad roads and in hilly country it is this animal that is chiefly useful, and the reason is that it is more sure-footed than the horse. In the hills there are often difficult passes, and ups and downs, where a foot misplaced means instant death.[1] It is this poor beast alone that in such places bears its load in safety to the stage's end. Its foal is [*hotā hai* and not *hai*] pretty, and active as well. It is very frisky, but as soon as the calamity of work falls on it, its promising shape and beauty are destroyed. If it were well cared for, its good looks would not be destroyed.[2] The fact is, it works all day; no thought of recreation, no trace of play. When the ass gives birth, she produces only one foal at a time.

If there is ever any talk of some one's folly, this poor creature is named first. What we have said refers to the baggage-ass only, for the wild ass is different; it is very swift. One species of wild ass is found in Sindh and Baluchistan and on the western border of the Panjab; it is called the *gor-khar*.[3] It is handsome and a reddish (*surkhī liye*)

[1] Two Preterites coupled by *aur*.

[2] *Khāk meṅ milnā.*

[3] For the Persian *gūr-i-khar*.

khākī in colour, but its face, breast and under parts are white, and down the length of its back it has a brown stripe.[1]

Horses and asses are hoofed (*sum-dār*) animals. Their hoofs are whole [2] (uncloven) and not cloven like the hoofs of animals that chew the cud.

[1] Called *selī* by horse-dealers; a 'list.' [2] *Sābit*.

27. THE DOG.

Wherever ten human habitations are found, there a dog too will surely be found, and its excellences are such that its presence cannot be regarded but as a boon. No animal is so gentle, so intelligent, and so affectionate. It is the gentleman's door-keeper, the shepherd's guardian, the sportsman's assistant.

Its understanding is excellent: it can be trained to do anything it is taught. Poverty and riches are alike to it. It sticks to anyone to whom it has once attached itself.[1] It may get badly fed on dry crusts, but it will not desert the house to which it belongs or go to the houses of the rich to get good food. In evil times it is [2] a comrade to its master, and should occasion arise,[3] it will even give up its life for him. This good animal always remembers the good done to it and forgets the evil. If its benefactor does any injury (too) to it, it does not remember it; should he then [immediately after injuring it] call it, it will come to him wagging its tail. A minute later it will lick the hand that beat it.

See; it appears from the picture that a mother has left her child asleep on a *chār-pā,ī* and gone somewhere on business. The wolf has seized the child by its clothes and has dragged it away a little; but the faithful house-dog is coming to save it. I am certain it will save it, as related in the following story:—

[1] *Jiskā ho-rahā*——; note idiom.

[2] Why *rahtā hai* and not *hai*? 'Vide' *Hindustani Stumbling-Blocks*. XXXI.

[3] *Waqt paṛe par*; note idiom.

A certain person was a keen sportsman. He kept [1] a dog of which he was very fond [2] and which was his constant companion. One day he went out shooting [3] and left the dog at home. On account of the dog's absence, he did not enjoy himself. In the evening when he returned, the dog ran to him wagging its tail as soon as it saw him. The master noticed that the dog's mouth and paws were covered with blood. When he went [4] into the house, he saw spots of blood everywhere.

This person had a smallish child. He looked for it here and there, but could not see it anywhere. He shouted, but still it did not make any sound. He thought [5] the dog had certainly killed the child. He was much grieved. Drawing his sword he ran at the dog crying out, "Oh cruel beast (*lit.* tyrant)! thou hast done an awful deed [6] and devoured [7] the darling of my heart."[8] The poor dog lay down and looked at him as though it were saying, "Pity, Pity!" But the world had become black in its master's eyes; he struck the dog such a blow with his sword that it gave one cry and just died.[9] The child was sleeping in another room, and started out of sleep at the dog's yell and began to cry. The master was astonished and went to it. When he looks, behold the child is alive and well, lying on its bed (*lit.* bedding), and a wolf is lying dead beside it. It was evident that the wolf had entered [10] the house with the intention of devouring the child, and that it was the dog that had killed it and saved the child's life. (The

1 *Pāl-rakhnā.* 2 *Pyār karnā.*

3 *Shikār* is any kind of sport; even bird-catching is included in the term.

4 "Came" as it was his own house. *Gayā* for a stranger's house.

5 After "thought," direct narration.

6 *Ghazab*, "wrath." For common idioms with *ghazab* and *balā* 'vide' *Hindustani Manual.*

7 *Phār-khānā*, "to tear and eat": meaning of both verbs retained.

8 *Kalejī* (lit. "liver") is metaphorically "heart."

9 *Dam tornā*, "to die." Note idioms.

10 *Ghusnā*, "to enter by force, or hurriedly."

man) quickly took the child in his lap. He was very sorry for what he had done, but what then was [1] the use of regret?

You will generally see that in cold countries, dogs have long and thick hair, and in hot countries short hair.

Wherever God places anyone to live, He gives him suitable [2] means for living there; for who would give [3] the poor things quilts and mattresses in cold climates?

The dog's activity and power of running are wonderful. Very many swift wild animals are its 'quarry.' [4] Hares and foxes are lucky if they escape from it. It tracks up its quarry by scent from a distance, and following up a scent digs the animal out of the ground; but it is necessary to train it to do these things. In our country no one bothers about dogs, but in England people keep various breeds of dogs and train them for various purposes, and they have discovered what breed is best for any particular purpose. Some are [5] watch-dogs, some remain with the flocks of sheep, some are for hunting the fox, and some for hunting the hare. The Hound [6] will follow up a 'quarry' (*shikār*) by scent when it flees from it, and make its master catch it. In the mountains, if travellers get swallowed up by the snow, dogs get them out. If you throw something light into the water, dogs will fetch it out. Some dogs have rescued drowning men. There is one breed of dog such that, if you show it any article and then secretly hide the article somewhere and an hour later, having walked several miles, give it an order [7] to go and bring the article, the dog will go and search and find out that article, wherever it may be. In some countries dogs are harnessed in carts and draw them pretty well; as many as thirty [8] dogs are harnessed in a cart.

[1] Ho*tā thā* not *thā*—why ?

[2] *Waise hī sāmān*: this use of *waise hī* is colloquial.

[3] *Lit.* "would have given (if——) ?"

[4] *Shikār.*

[5] *Ko,ī—hai.* *Ko,ī* requires a singular verb.

[6] *Bū-dar kutta*, any dog that hunts by scent.

[7] Direct narration.

[8] *Tīs tīs.*

28. THE CAT.

The cat has a heart-felt attachment to man (pl.). Like the dog (pl.), it too becomes very familiar. It lives in men's houses boldly, and without fear (*lit.* danger). It is always so gentle that children play with it. It takes and eats a fallen bone or a bit of meat, and lives on that. It is a very very clean animal [three adjectives] and is always cleaning itself.[1] Its mouth and its rough tongue are, for it, water and towel. It licks and wets its paw and with it cleans its face and ears and other parts that its tongue cannot reach [*lit.* its face or ears, whatever cannot be reached by its tongue, it having licked and wetted its hand, by it, having rubbed and rubbed, cleans (them)[2]]. The cat has soft (*narm narm*)[3] hair. In some countries fur coats (*postīn*) are made of its skin (*post*). The Kabul (*Wilāyatī*) cat is very handsome and for this reason is costly.[4] This breed comes from Kabul and Persia. As a rule it is pure-white (*yak-rang safed*): it has much long hair (*pashm*, lit. "wool"), soft as silk. There are several species of wild cats, differing in colour and size. Some are very handsome. Some are from 2½ to 3 feet in length.

The eyes of cats are of an unusual kind; they can see well in the dark. They hunt, by means of these eyes, rats, mice and other animals which do not come out by day. When the cat is lying dozing (*ūṅghnā*) in the sun (sunshine), how quiet and gentle it appears with its low purring; but if opportunity offers, it becomes ferocious (*sher*). Just look at its tiny teeth; how fine and sharp they are! Hold[5] its paw a little in your hand; how soft it is! You will think that there is nothing harmful in it. Wait a bit—don't let go yet. If it is at all

[1] *Badan ṣāf karnā*; note this way of expressing a reflexive verb.

[2] Note the order and construction in the original, and learn by heart.

[3] *Narm narm*, soft throughout.

[4] Many 'Persian cats' are brought to India by Kabulis.

[5] *Thāmnā*, "to hold in the hand." *Pakaṛnā*, generally means "to catch."

worried, then from these soft paws what lancet-like claws come out suddenly (——*paṛnā*)!

Its claws are long, and crooked, and sharp at the points. If they remained projecting like a dog's, it would be difficult for the cat to get about, and the claws too would not keep so sharp. It puts them out when necessity arises, and when it likes draws them in again.

It is a strange sight to see it hunt a bird.[1] See, see, how quietly with silent foot-fall (*dabe pā,oṅ se*) it stalks in the bushes. How very quietly it places its soft paws, without the sound even of a foot-fall. There it is lying in ambush behind the trunk. What a poor simple bird that is! See, its prey has come within its reach (*zad* or *mār*). There (*wuh*), the cat has pounced on it, and in one spring[2] has caught it (*jā-liyā*). Oh, oh (*ay hay*)! How the poor thing flutters! Look at the cat's face; how distorted its expression is! How changed its eyes are!

Indians name the cat 'the school-mistress of the tiger,' and tell[3] this story about it:—It taught the tiger all its skill (*kartab*).[4] At last the tiger said (asked), "Aunt Cat; is there anything remaining to be learnt?" The cat gathered that the tiger's intention was evil. It humbly replied, "That's all, my son; there's nothing more." The tiger wished to prey on the cat first. It ran to the attack. There was a tree near. The cat at once climbed up it, and the tiger was left looking foolishly on.

Many animals have claws concealed in their paws,[5] which they cause to protrude at will. These are all meat-eating animals, and prefer the meat of prey killed by themselves. Their teeth are specially suited for preying. Their tongue

[1] Note the construction of the original.

[2] *Chhalāng*, f., (*mārnā*), a long jump.

[3] *Gha nā*, to make up (of news, reports, etc.).

[4] *Kartab*, m., "achievement, deed; skill"; but *kartūt*, m., "bad deeds."

[5] Retractile.

is rough, and if any meat remains adhering to the bone (pl.), they scrape it off with it. These animals all walk on their toes.[1]

[1] Digitigrade as opposed to plantigrade.

29. THE MONGOOSE.

Just look near that bush: a mongoose and a snake are battling together. The mongoose is very cute. It has gripped the snake's neck in its mouth so firmly that the poor thing's tongue is hanging out. The snake (too) has wound itself round the mongoose's neck [*lit.* has become the necklace of the mongoose's throat], but what can it do? It is helpless; its enemy has found its opportunity. Look at the mongoose; how it enjoys chewing the snake's neck! In a short time it will make an end of the snake.[1] Then it will watch for other prey (*shikār*).

The mongoose is a very adventurous animal. Its lips are very red, as though it had [2] chewed betel. Look at its body; how active it is; it can run very fast. [3] It silently waits in ambush, and when the time comes, springs up, and jumps forward, and rushes at [4] its prey. It is always alert. It sits up on its hind legs and looks about it so that one can't help laughing.[5] Its teeth are sharp. It hunts and eats many small animals but it likes mice best.

Its colour is *k͟hākī* and hence the poor animals it hunts do not notice its approach. It captures its prey by surprise. If its prey is not in sight, it tracks it out. Like a well-trained dog, it hunts and searches in every corner and finds it out. It hunts for and eats the eggs of grey-partridges and quails, etc., which nest on the ground. It is an enemy [*lit.* great tyrant] to hens and pigeons, breaking their necks and drinking their blood. It also kills rats, mice, various small snakes, and lizards.

[1] *Sāṅp kā kām tamām ho-jā,egā.*
[2] "Has chewed."
[3] *Dauṛne meṅ bahut chālāk.*
[4] *Jhapaṭ-kar ḥamla karnā.*
[5] *Haṅsī ānā.*

30. THE SPIDER.

This hunts[1] by great strategy.[2] It spins many webs so fine that the eye cannot discover them. There, in some corner, it remains crouching. If a moth or a fly is snared in its net, it is dead[3] (a gone coon). What a beautiful web it spins: on seeing it one's brain is bewildered.

Right in the centre of the web, this spider is sitting. It has caught a fly. How it enjoys eating it! Another spider, on the look-out for prey, is waiting (sitting) in a corner.

How should tiny insects[4] know that a tyrant is thirsting for their blood [*lit.* to tiny tiny animals what knowledge[5] that, "A tyrant thirsting for our blood is seated?"].

Should anything fly into the web and get entangled, the spider will pounce on it like a tiger and hug it [*lit.* whatever[6] will come flying and will be entangled in the web, this one will rush on like a tiger—], and will make an end of the poor helpless creature on the spot.

Listen! The spider attaches[7] a very little gum to the spot where she sits, and lets herself down, and as she descends she keeps on paying out a thread. When the thread is a yard or so[8] in length, she stops and begins to swing, and by continued swinging, swings up to[9] a branch of another tree. Now there is a 'clothes-line' stretched tight between two trees. By means of the thread, the spider goes to and fro, and thus, weaving warp and woof, makes her web.

In the evening many tiny insects fly about[10] for pleasure. They don't see the web [*lit.* to them the web does not appear].

1 *Shikār khelnā.*

2 *Ghāt lagānā*, to lie in ambush.

3 Note idiom.

4 *Jānwar.*

5 *Khabar*, "information."

6 Note this construction and imitate it.

7 *Lit.* "The spider, *where* she sits, *there* she attaches ——." Note construction.

8 *Lit.* one yard, half a yard.

9 *Jā-lagtī hai.*

10 *Uṛnā phirnā*, note use of two verbs for an English verb and adverb.

As soon as they come, they are snared.[1] The spider, sitting quietly at home, gets fresh prey every day.

You must have seen that some spiders are very small[2] and skip about.[3] If (or when[4]) they are hungry, they crouch and lie flat[5] on the ground, keeping on the watch.[6] As soon as a fly comes and settles before it, the spider very slowly begins to move, and keeping close to the ground all the time[7] advances, so stealthily that the fly is not the least aware (*makkhī ko khabar bhī nahīṅ*) of the movement. When the fly is within springing distance, the spider pounces on it like a tiger, and hugs it [*lit. where* the fly remained a spring's distance off *and* the spider pounced on it like a tiger and hugged[8] it]. In some spiders a poison is found like that in snakes. When they hunt flies or other various small insects, the insects die of their bite.

1 Note idiom.

2 "Very small" and not "smallish," as *makṛi* itself is small, smaller than *makṛā*. 'Vide' *Hindustani Stumbling-Blocks*.

3 *Uchalnā phirnā*; 'vide' note 10, page 34.

4 'If' and 'when' are both "conditional particles."

5 *Chipaknā.*

6 *Tāk lagā,e baiṭhnā.*

7 Note the force of the repetitions.

8 The two Preterites coupled by "and" signify concomitance; *vide* Hind. Man. and Hind. Stumbling-Blocks.

31. THE ANT.

What a tiny body! What perseverance! It lifts a load the double of itself. It does not avoid work or shirk labour. How it exhausts itself.[1] With what great labour (*lit.* misfortune) does it earn its living! See God's power. What a marvellous memory! How far afield it travels and still does not forget the way back.[2]

It is devoted to sweet things, but still it doesn't pass by other things. See; there's a wasp lying dead. To ants, it is a *shikār*. How they cling[3] to it! One pulls at the wings, another drags

1 *Jān khapānā.* 2 *Ṭhikāna nahīṅ bhūlnā.* 3 Preterite.

at the body; one clings to the head and another hugs a leg. One is flying; the poor thing's death is near. "Why, it's well and strong; how do you know it will die?" "When their wings appear, the day of death is near for them. Have you never heard the proverb, 'The Ant's wings have appeared'? This is said when (*lit.* where) anyone boasts of wealth and power, and death overtakes him. A good trait in ants is that if any one of them finds anything, it tells the whole, and whatever they find they divide and eat together."

Come into the garden and watch [1] them. See how that army of ants is marching in file.[2] They look as though going on some important expedition.[3] Look; in what a straight line they move, not one straying from the road [*lit.* is there any power, possibility, that any should stray from the road hither or thither?]. Just as their feet are very tiny, so they leave a very fine track. Some are carrying eggs: some are unencumbered.

This one, that is going the opposite way, is travelling as though it had [4] forgotten something. It sometimes moves to the right of the *qaṭār*, and sometimes to the left, but it never leaves it. Sometimes it stops, and joining its face to the one that meets it (*sāmne-wālā*), it takes its way again. It is as though it had stopped to say something. Come let us go ahead a bit and look. Where are all these going? *Bhā,ī*! in the open they were visible but here in the grass all have vanished from sight. Come a little further on still, they will certainly be visible in these flower-beds. Look, they are keeping to the edge of the beds. See how they avoid the clods and plants in the bed! How will they avoid this large branch that has been cut off and is lying here? See, they cross over the branch pretty easily.

A clear straight road lay before them; why did they not go by it? There is a pool of water and they made a detour in

1 —*kī sair karnā* of inanimate things; but *sair dekhnā*, of animate things.

2 *Qaṭār*, file; *or* line one behind the other.

3 *Muhimm.*

4 "May have forgotten."

order to follow its brink. Now they have arrived at the root of an old tree, and here they will disappear (also). All have descended into this narrow split and are travelling along it. Evening has come and our eyes can't see.[1] Let us go home.

There are many more strange things about the ants, but they are difficult to explain; hence have been omitted here.

[1] *Nigāh kām nahīṅ kartī. Jahāṅ tak nigāh kām kartī hai*=" as far as the eye can reach.

32. SUGAR-CANE.

See, a sugar-cane seller [1] is sitting under the tree. His basket is before him and in his hand is the cutter (*sarotā*). He is cutting joints of sugar-cane (*gaṇḍerī*). A boy is seated there buying sugar-cane. The other has completed his purchase. In one hand he is holding a handkerchief full of *gaṇḍerīs*, while with the other he is picking them out and sucking them. There is a very tiny child in the lap of a woman, and a very small girl is with her. The girl has seen the sugar-cane and is extending (*phailā rakhā hai*) one hand towards it. With the other hand she is tugging at her mother, entreating her to buy her some sugar-cane.

Sugar-cane is one of the great blessings (*ni'mat*) of India.

In the Panjab, sugar-cane intended for planting (*lit.* sowing) is cut in *Māgh* (January) and buried in a pit to protect it from cold. In *Phāgan* (February) or *Chait* (March), each cane is cut into lengths of about a quarter of a yard, and buried in the planting field. From each joint several branches sprout out and those branches become sugar-cane. White-ants and insects attack it, and rats too do a great deal of mischief to it.

There are many varieties of sugar-cane of which the *paunḍā* [2] is most used for eating.

The cane ripens in eight or nine months and is then crushed in a press. Every day the juice that is expressed is boiled.

[1] *Gaṇḍerī*, a joint of sugar-cane, and *gaṇḍeryā*, a seller of it.

[2] *Paunḍā*, a thick kind, of good flavour.

If *guṛ* has to be made, the juice is dried. If *rāb* [1] has to be made, they keep it thick (and don't let it dry).

From the *rāb* they make *shakar* [2] and from the *shakar*, *khāṅḍ* [3], *qand*, [4] and *misṛī* ; [5] and from these again sweets are made, which are eaten by all, rich or poor.

1 *Rāb*, Hind., "inspissated juice (of the sugar-cane), treacle, molasses, syrup."

2 *Shakar*, f., and *chīnī* are confused terms applied to different kinds of sugar in different parts.

3 *Khāṅḍ*, f., common brown sugar.

4 *Qand*, m., loaf sugar (in cones).

5 *Misṛī*, f., sugar-candy.

33. THE MANGO.

Just look in front of you. How many [1] mango trees there are! Those on the near side appear large, but those on the far side [2] appear small. There's a man too going along under the trees. On his head is a bundle. He is steadying [3] it with his right hand. On his shoulder is a stick. With the top end of it he keeps supporting [4] the bundle. The bottom end he keeps depressed by his hand. There are two goats also. One has its head bent down eating grass; the other has turned its head round and is watching him.

The mango fruit is common in India. See its many excellences: the tree is handsome and it is shady; the unripe fruit even is useful; the ripe too is useful. If it is unripe, *chaṭnī* is made of it, and pickles and preserves, [5] and hundreds of maunds of *āmchūr* are made [5] by drying it. When it is ripe, people slice it and eat it, or else suck it.

In the Panjab its season of enjoyment [*lit.* Spring] begins in the months of *Chait* and *Baisakh* (March and April). Then (*phir*), if you look at the tree it is laden with *maur* (mango-blossom). When the *maur* falls, many tiny green fruits are visible.

1 *Kitne sāre*, pl.

2 Note *ure* (vulgar for *ware*), and *pare*.

3 Past Participle to signify state: *pakaṛnā*.

4 *Sahārā de-rakhnā*. Perfect Tense.

5 *Āchār ḍālnā* or *banānā* : 'vide' *Hind. Man.*, p. 157 (*d*).

When they grow in size, squirrels and parrots feed on them. Most trees produce quantities of fruit, but when a storm comes so much fruit falls (*jhaṛnā*) that the ground is carpeted.[1] Still the trees appear to be laden.

When (*jahāṅ*) colour comes on the fruit, whole flocks of parrots begin to settle (fall) on them. Oh heartless *mālī*! Certainly the parrots *do* injure your property, still don't 'pellet' them, lest the wings of the poor things get broken (and they fall to the ground), and flutter and die.

The grafted trees have a peculiar beauty of their own. Each is quite a small plant bearing five or six mangoes of a pound weight each, and by their weight the branches touch the ground. The mango bears one year so much fruit that it with difficulty can support it; the next year so very few mangoes appear that men and animals both long for them. Some trees fruit only every other year, while some bear all the year round and these are called *bārah-māsyā*.[2]

The mango is as much liked by children as by old men and youths. If you once give a slight taste (*lit.* lick) of one to an infant,[3] it will never leave you alone. As soon as it sees a mango it will stretch out its hand.[4] The koel [5] and the mango come together. As soon as the mangoes begin to colour, the koel arrives. When the mangoes are over, it departs to other countries. In the rainy season how pleasant the koel's voice sounds from a distance.

1 *Bichaunā (ho jātā hai)*; m.

2 Bārah, "twelve," and *māsa*, S., "a month."

3 *Dūdh pītā (hū,ā) bachcha.* Muslim children are suckled up till two years, and in practice often up till four.

4 *Hāth dauṛānā.*

5 *Ko,el,* the Indian Ko,el, a species of Cuckoo. The male is black and has bright crimson eyes.

34. THE NEEM.[1]

The houses of Indians are seldom airy (*hawā-dār*). For them the *nīm* tree takes the place of an airy room. Little sunshine

1 *Nīm*, the Neem or Margosa Tree, *Melia Azadirachta.*

filters through into the shade cast by a *nīm* tree Its foliage is so dense that its small branches are hidden; the small birds chirp loudly but remain concealed. It blossoms freely and the neighbouring houses are pervaded with the perfume.

The *nīm* is as well known in India for its bitterness as the sugar-cane for its sweetness; but just as much as it is bitter it has sweet qualities to counteract its bitterness. Its leaves, bark, blossom, and fruit are all useful in medicine.

Nīm wood, when it is old, is no whit inferior to *shīsham* for hardness, and its chief excellence is that weevils do not attack it; moreover if clothes are kept in chests made of it, or if its leaves are placed with books or *pashmīna*,[1] insects will not attack them. When the *nīm* tree gets very old, moisture begins to ooze out of one of its branches and this they call *mad*[2] People tie small earthen pots (*hāndī*) underneath and collect the *mad* and keep it[3] in bottles.

[1] *Pashmīna*, a soft stuff made of fine goat-hair. *Pashm*, P., "wool."

[2] *Mad*, another name for *tāṛī* or toddy.

[3] *Bhar-rakhnā* = *bharkar rakhnā*.

35. THE DATE-PALM.

In the dry, sandy, and waste (*banjar*) parts of India, this tree abounds. It grows quickly in such soil and fruits quickly too in places where (*us jagah—jahāṅ*) other plants survive with difficulty. In villages, beams of *kachchā* houses are made from this tree. Out of the leaves, matting and hand-fans are made. The fibre of the leaves is woven into baskets and matting, and ropes too are made of it. In many parts of India the young central leaves, before opening, are gathered and cooked and eaten as greens.

36. THE HOT WEATHER.

Come, let me show you a picture of the hot weather. In the arch over the doorway a parrot-cage is suspended.

Under it a man is sitting napping. A *ḥuqqa* is in front of him. The rope of a *bahangī* [1] (bangy) is in his hand.

"What is in the *bahangī*?"

"*Ṣurāḥīs* of water."

"Why has he put them there?"

"To cool the water."

"How is it cooled?"

"One man pulls the rope and the *bahangī* swings. The air strikes the *ṣurāḥīs* and by this means the water is quickly cooled."

"Who is on the bed with the mosquito curtains?"

"A Babu is lying on it. He is much distressed (*be-tāb*) by the heat. He has removed his *pagṛī* and placed it at the foot of his bedstead. His right hand is on his knee and in his left hand is a fan. A servant is standing by fanning him: by much fanning he has become tired: his head (*lit.* neck) is on one side."

Oh the heat! As the sun (*lit.* sunshine) rises, so do people's faces decline. How hot the wind became the moment the sun rose. One's eyes cannot see on account of the glare. One's brain won't work [2] clear whether one writes or reads. Sweat flows; the flies tease; heaven and earth are burning; the trees are yellow; when the poor birds choke they open their beaks, and to escape the sun (sunshine) they bury themselves in the branches.

A traveller is going along in a *maidān*. The sun falls on him from above and the ground under him burns. If he finds anywhere the shade of a tree he thinks he has reached Heaven. But if the hot wind (*lū*) blows, the shade of no tree is of use, nor the shadow of an umbrella. Small children are in a bad way (*lit.* strange state). Their flower-like faces are withered, their complexions are pale (*lit.* yellow). The

[1] *Bahangī* is a long pole with a net suspended at each end: used for carrying loads.

[2] *Hosh ṭhikāne na-honā*, lit. "the senses not being in their proper places."

cup is no sooner away from their lips than they cry for water. In no way can their thirst be quenched.

Those to whom God has given, sometimes have by day *ṭaṭṭīs* sprinkled with water, or else they plunge into cellars. At night they sleep on the roof. Flowers are sprinkled on their beds. Punkahs are swung. They toss about crying (*ki*), "Oh how hot it is![1] My whole body[2] is being burnt."

[1] Lit. "*Hā,e*, the air is hot."

[2] *Tan badan* both mean "body."

37. THE COLD WEATHER.

The Rains are over and the Cold Weather has come. The tanks are drying up ; the rivers have gone down and become mere streams or *nālās*. The days have shortened and the nights lengthened. The weather (air) is getting cooler. Now neither will the frogs croak nor the mosquitos worry. The snakes have gone into their holes and the lizards are skulking in the crannies of the walls. Now many kinds of birds are migrating to hot countries and other birds are taking their place. The cold weather is pleasing to (*bhānā*) geese, cranes, and water-fowl. They are coming in, in long lines, and settling in (*ābād karnā*) the jungles, the streams, and the jheels.

Just (*ẕarā*) look at the picture. A line of camels is marching down a hill road. The Kabulis[1] are bringing fruits of Afghanistan, and will sell them in many big towns. Just (*to*) look at the faces (*ṣūrat*) of these Kabulis! How fierce they look! Much long hair—a face red all over—very dirty loose flowing garments. These people sell horses as well. Their horses are small in size but very strong.

At this season most Government Officers make their tours, and the village cultivators make (*sunānā*) their complaints and obtain justice. The Inspectors of Schools, too, at this season,

[1] *Wilāyat*, a foreign country, hence Kabul, hence England. *Wilāyatī* for men always means *Kabuli*, but *wilāyatī chīz* means "English goods." *Wilāyatī anār* of course means *Kabul* pomegranates.

make their tours and examine the village children. At this season, too, regiments march in relief, marching one stage a day; they make many long marches. By the daily exercise and fresh air (*hawā khānā*) their health benefits [*lit.* they become very strong].

See how cold it has become the moment the sun has gone down. Come, let us sit indoors and light the fire, and toast ourselves, and repeat our lessons learnt in class (*sabaq yād karnā*), and prepare our lessons for to-morrow (*muṭāla'a dekhnā*).

Some poor creatures pass these nights in the open. They remain squatting round a bonfire under their blankets [1] and shiver with the cold: their teeth chatter. When the sun comes out, some life comes into their bodies.

In these days snow falls.[2] Snow is [3] very soft and light. For many months at a time many high mountains remain covered by it. Sometimes even the passes become white. In such places the streams (springs) freeze, and become so hard that people can walk about on them.

When Spring comes, a slight warmth is felt in the air. The bare trees become green and fresh. Flowers blossom. How beautiful their lovely colours appear to the eyes! Wherever you look it is a beautiful sight. Spring is seen everywhere.[4] Something like life is returning to the birds. They are singing out in their glee. The *Shāmā* and the *Ko,el* are on the mango trees and ravish one's heart with their many sweet notes. The wasps fly [5] about here and there and make their combs. The cultivators plough. Rice is sown. The wheat begins[6] to ripen. If a few drops of rain fall now, the *zamīn-dārs* are much pleased.

1 *Kammal oṛhnā. Pahinnā* "to wear," refers to *cut* garments only or to boots, hats, etc.

2 *Paṛtī hai.* Why not *paṛ-rahī hai*? 3 Why *hotī hai* and not *hai*?

4 *Bahār hī bahār*, Spring and only Spring.

5 Expressed in Hindustani by two verbs.

6 *Pakne par ānā* "to be about to—," *not* usually "to begin to—." *Yih kitāb khatm hone par ā,ī* "this book is nearly finished."

38. THE RAINS.

The Hot Weather is gone and the Rains have come. See, what a black heavy cloud has arisen: this will certainly bring rain [*lit.* will not remain without raining]. By all means open the door; there is no hot wind blowing now. Just come outside and see what a very cool breeze is blowing. Ah, there is thunder;[1] there, now it lightens; there, too, drops of rain have begun to fall. Just see how all in a moment (*ān hī ān meṅ*) the season has changed.[2]

To-day one should think about the mind of the cultivators.[3] How delighted they must be. Look, Sir! it is now raining cats and dogs; the gutters are flowing profusely.

Our souls have been longing for a breath of cool air; to-day for the first time for some months we shall be able to sleep in comfort (—*sonā naṣīb hogā*). If this state of things (i.e., rain) continues, [4] nothing but green (*sabza hī sabza*) will be seen in the jungle.

The rain has now stopped. Come, let us go for a walk in the jungle.[5] See how cloudless the sky has become. Oh, the rainbow! Just look! What various (*kyā kyā*) colours it has. Just listen [6] —how joyously the *ko,el* is "kūking." To-night too the *papīhās* [7] will twitter and all the songsters of the Rains will sing. Hallo! what's that? That's a frog. Bother (*tauba*, lit. "repentance")! they are croaking and filling the whole jungle with their din.

Look at the trees! How clean they have been washed. Just look at that part (*kinārā*) of the sky. Who can count

[1] *Garjā* from *garajnā* ; *bādal* understood.

[2] *Mausim phirnā.*

[3] Plural in Urdu idiom.

[4] Preterite Tense in a condition. It assumes the completion of the condition.

[5] *Jangal kī sair karnā.* *Jangal* means not only forest and jungle, but also wilderness, *i.e.*, anything opposed to habitation.

[6] *Sunnā.* Why Infinitive? 'Vide' *Hindustani Manual.*

[7] The *papīhā* says, *pī kahān* "where is my master?"

the colours of these clouds? Just look, the red-velvet insects have come out. The birds will tire [1] themselves by picking up and eating so many insects.

1 Physically tired. But *ām khāne se jī bhar-gayā* "I'm tired of eating mangoes."

39. THE COCK.

The cock is a very brave and handsome bird. When he swaggers along erect at the head of his hens, it is as though he well knew [1] he was a Somebody—and how swaggeringly he is walking! When he sits on a wall or a stone or a mound, he looks like a very hero of 'Thirty-at-a-Blow.' [2] He fills his throat, throws out his chest, and cries with all his might, "Cock-a-doodle-do" (*kukuṛūṅ-kūṅ*) as though to tell (*sunānā*) the whole world what a dandy and hero he is. He is death on a fight.[3] Sometimes heartless people amuse themselves at the expense of his quarrelsome habits. They are not content even with his natural weapons, i.e., his spurs, but mount the spurs with sharp iron and release him in front of an adversary similarly equipped.

The domestic hen lays many eggs, which are excellent eating. She patiently sits on her eggs for twenty-one days and hatches them. She defends her young with the greatest boldness. If dogs or cats approach her house (*daṛbā* fowl-house), she puffs up her feathers and runs at them clucking [4] in anger. From her terrifying aspect (*ḍarā,onī ṣūrat*), it seems as though she were ready to kill or be killed; only an adventurous animal would now face her. If a kite comes hovering over her young, she at once hides them under her wings. The chickens are very pretty—pink legs—round black eyes shining like stars—clad in soft hairy coats of yellow and white—they run about 'cheeping.'

1 Direct narration.

2 "Seven-at-a-Blow."—*Grimm's Fairy Tales.*

3 "Ever spoiling for a fight." Note idiom.

4 *Kurkurānā*, to cluck. *Kuruk murg͟hī*, "a broody hen."

40. THE VULTURE.

Just look ahead of you. How many vultures are collected together. Hallo! there is a dead bullock there or the carcass of an ass, for vultures subsist on such flesh as this. How objectionable and terrifying their appearance is! Huge in size, with dirty brown feathers, bare necks, bald heads, curved beaks, and widely-opened eyes. What disgusting animals they are! What filthy (*g͟halīẓ*) things they eat with a relish! They are so engaged on their food (*g͟hiẕā*) that they only [1] know of our approach when we are on the top of them. Then they abandon their feast with regret. Spreading their broad wings they silently take wing. They go to no great distance but settle on the trees round about so that their beloved food should not be screened (*ojhal*) from their view. When they get an opportunity, they will at once come back. This bird is a great glutton (*khā,ū*) and wants [2] to fill itself up to its nostrils. When its belly is filled full, it goes and sits on a tree on some very high rock (*patthar*). It shuts its eyes and remains sitting there looking half-dead (*ādh mū,ā-sā*) till its objectionable nutriment (*g͟hiẕā*) is digested.

Very many [3] birds eat grain and insects; but the vulture eats meat only (*gosht hī*). It is a bird of prey, though dead things (*murdār*) are more pleasing to it than *shikār*. The Goshawk, the Indian Sparrow-Hawk, the Peregrine, the Lagar Falcon, the Kite,[4] the Owl, etc., are all birds of prey.

1 *Jabhī*. Note idiom.

2 Direct narration.

3 *Bahut se*—.

4 These are all females. The males or 'tiercels' have different names. The English Sparrow-Hawk is the *bāsha*.

41. THE SPARROW.

This is a well-known bird, all know it. There can be no one in India who in his childhood has not heard stories of Mr. and Mrs. Sparrow. Whatever season you look for it, you will find it round about the house (pl.). In fact it has a natural (*qudratī*) attachment to man (pl.); where he dwells, *there* is it to be found. It lives happily everywhere, whether in bazars amongst crowds, or outside in the open air amongst desolation (*sunsān*). Its plumage is not gay (*shokh*) but monkishly plain (*ṣūfiyāna*); but still it has a style (*shān*), and the blending of the colours in its feathers is not unpleasing. Just look at its eyes, how bright and shining they are! What a strong beak: the point is sharp. The cock sparrow is quite a small bird, but still he is very pugnacious, and so bold and impudent (*ḍhīṭ*), there is scarcely anything it is afraid of.

42. THE HOOPOE [1] OR THE 'CARPENTER.'

Look at this; sometimes it is on one branch of the tree and sometimes on the other. How handsome it is! Its flame-coloured crest (*tāj*) is shining in the sun (sunshine). How black is each point of the feathers in its "crown." Look; on its back, too, to match them, are three black stripes. Its broad wings too are handsome. On them are black and white stripes, and these give it an additional beauty (*bahār*). But what is worth seeing is its beak, long, thin, and curved. This is put to very many useful purposes. By means of [2] this beak, it extracts the insects concealed in the ground or in old and decayed [3] trees. It works thoughtfully and slowly. When it begins to eat, it pounds the insects with its beak and makes them into a kind of dough. Strange to say, the beaks of its young are not crooked, nor have they any necessity for being crooked. The parent birds bring food and feed them, but as the young grow big and begin to feed themselves, so their beaks become curved.

[1] It is auspicious (*mubārak*), and reverenced by Muslims. It is the bird of Solomon. Translators of the Qur'ān have confused it with the Lapwing.

[2] Why *ba-daulat*?

[3] *Gale saṛe* = very rotten, from *galnā*, to dissolve, go to pieces; and *saṛnā*, to rot.

The hoopoe nests in hollow trees and in holes in walls ; it furnishes (*sajānā*) its home with bits of grass and feathers. It lays from four to seven eggs; their colour is bluish white.

People have made up many strange tales about its "crown." Egyptians call it the son of King Solomon and they tell a story about it, that formerly its "crown" was of real gold, and through greed (*lālach*) people were in the habit of killing it. It complained to *Ḥaẓrat Sulaymān* and brought forward its case. Solomon knew that its crown was the pest of its life, and that as long as that remained on its head, greedy people would continue to kill [1] it. He ordered the crown to turn into feathers, and from that time its gold departed (flew away) and feathers took its place.

People have made up many other stories like the previous one about its crown. If you ask me the truth, what *is* worth noticing (*khiyāl karnā*), is its beak, as has already been stated.

[1] *Mārtā-rahnā* (in the Future).

43. THE SNAKE.

Have a care! Don't walk with bare feet in this long grass, lest (*aisā na ho ki*) you accidentally [1] put your foot on a snake. It is a fact that not all snakes are poisonous, but in India there are many poisonous snakes, so one should be cautious.[2] Don't judge them (*—par na-jānā*) by their small size ;[3] they are very noxious (*mūẕī*). A man bitten by a cobra generally dies within (*andar hī*) half an hour.

In this country there is a caste of people who state that they are snake-charmers.[4] They claim that by virtue (*zor*) of their spells, they can draw poisonous snakes out of their holes. They tease them, and play with them, and the snakes do not bite them at all. The fact is that the snakes with which they play, have been tamed.

[1] *Paṛ-jānā.* [2] *Hoshyār*, alert. [3] Note idiom.

[4] *Sāṅp kā mantrī.* *Mantar* is "a charm that is repeated;" originally "a verse in the Vedas"

44. THE TIGER.

This is a very handsome, proud, and powerful[1] animal. In some points it resembles the cat, the chītā, and the leopard, *i.e.*, its claws, too, like those of these animals, remain concealed within the paw and can be protruded at will. Its tongue too is rough, so that it may lick (scrape) off with it any meat that may adhere to the bone. Like the above-mentioned animals, it walks on its toes. Under the toes is soft flesh, so that when it walks, its foot-fall may be noiseless. It has eyes too like those animals, so that it sees equally well by day or by night. Its ears too are like theirs, so that if there is the least sound (*āhaṭ*) it at once hears it. Though the tiger cannot climb trees like the cat, still it is very active: it springs to a great distance. In its every movement (*adā*)[2] there is grace (*k͟hūsh-numā,ī*) and pride. Its colour is a deep but bright yellow, and on it are darkish stripes. The hair (*pashm*) of the belly, chest, and neck, is light coloured. A full-grown tiger generally measures from its head to the tip of its tail, nine, or nine and a half, feet. Some are even ten feet. A few have been found up to eleven or twelve feet.

The tiger is found in the jungles, forests, and low (small) hills of India, and generally keeps to dense thickets in long grass. Sometimes three or four are to be seen together on an old temple or on the walls of an old ruin. While (*yūṅ to*) tigers are to be found in other countries of Asia, still they are most abundant in India.

The tigress produces two to four at a litter, and generally gives birth in some spot in the jungle where the undergrowth is dense. The young remain with their mother until they can hunt for themselves.[3] The tigress has a great affection for her young. If anyone carries off her young, she stays hid in the neighbourhood for three or four nights in succession, roaring with rage.

1 *Shāh-zor*, only used of physical strength.

2 *Adā*, f., also "manner, *and* coquetry."

3 *Jab tak——nahiṅ kar-sakte*; *vide* "Hindustani Manual," p. 132 (*b*).

Four tiger cubs were found in the jungle by the servants of a ṣāḥib; they carried off two and presented them to their master (*āqā*). The master sent them to the stable where they remained crying several nights. At last the mother traced them out and she came so full of rage that it seemed she would destroy the whole stable. The master did not like to shoot a tigress with young but without killing her he could not keep the cubs. He was obliged to let the cubs go.

The tiger is very fond of preying on cattle (*—kā shikār karnā*), but it also kills wild pigs, *sāmbhar* deer, *chītal*, and other wild animals. The young full-grown tiger is a great tyrant and sometimes kills as many as four or five cows at once, but the old tiger generally kills only according to its requirements (*bhūkh ke muwāfiq*). The truth is the tiger is a cowardly animal. When any one confronts it, it retires. But of course (*hāṅ*) when wounded or enraged, it does not retire. It generally lies hidden by day, and by night lies in ambush for its prey, and when any animal comes to drink at a stream or a pond, it makes one spring and suddenly knocks it down. It sometimes happens that the tiger rushes at a wild boar, which rips it up with its long, sharp, and prominent tusks. Sometimes when a tiger attacks a herd of cattle, the herd does not fall a prey to it, but faces it and drives it back. It is stated in a book that once a herd of buffalos was grazing and with it was a herdsman's son. The tiger seized the boy. The whole of the buffalos rushed at the tiger and released the boy.

Once a tiger was not able to eat anything for many days and grew very thin. A shikārī shot it and found (saw) that a porcupine's quill had stuck in its throat. It must have caught a porcupine somewhere and a quill must have stuck in its throat, and so it could not swallow. The tiger prefers the flesh of animals slain by itself, but sometimes it will eat dead carcasses. Once a ṣāḥib shot a tigress and thought (knew) that she was dead. He returned to his tent and sent an elephant to bring in the dead tiger. The men returned and reported that the tiger was still alive. The next day, the ṣāḥib went himself. He saw that another tiger had dragged it off and had eaten about half. The ṣāḥib shot this tiger too.

The tiger does not usually attack man. In some parts of the Dakan it has happened that a tiger has come and carried off one or two villagers who were lying asleep in an open shed. It sometimes, too, happens that when a tiger grows old and its teeth become blunt and its strength departs, that it takes to killing men only, because man, compared to wild animals, is an easy prey.

You must certainly know that of the doomed persons (*maut kā mārā*) tigers capture, scarcely one ever escapes[1] death; but it has happened that some lucky persons' (*qismat-wālā*)[2] have got out of the clutches of this tyrant. On the occasion (*mauqiʻ*) of a war, six hundred soldiers were on the march and reached their halting-place rather late at night. There was a large jungle near the camp. The Commander was quite weary (*thakā māndа*) and wanted to have a few (*do chār*) hours' sleep; but no sooner did he lie down than he heard the report of a rifle. He started up and ran to the entrance of his tent and was questioning the sentry from which direction the shot had come, when suddenly (*ki itne meṅ*) a very big tiger, carrying a sepoy in its jaws, bounded past him crossing his front. The sentry immediately fired. The tiger gave a bound foreward and rushed off. The Commander, the sentry, and some other sepoys who came up, all ran after the tiger and tracked it for several hundred yards, by the blood here and there; but no one had hope about the poor sepoy. At that moment (*itne meṅ*) the tiger roared out, making the hills resound. Then about fifty yards off in the bushes a shout was[3] heard. When they advance and look,[4] behold the Muslim sepoy comes limp-

[1] What is the difference between *chhūṭnā* and *bachnā*?

[2] *Iqbāl-wālā* "prosperous."

[3] What are all the meanings of *lalkārnā*? Frame short sentences illustrating them.

[4] Aorist for Historical Present; *vide* "Hindustani Stumbling-Blocks," XXXVI, 7 (*a*).

ing towards them. They questioned him (*ḥāl daryāft karnā*), and learnt that the poor fellow had carried food to the picquet and was returning, when (*ki*) he heard a rustling. Before he could turn round and look,[1] a tiger knocked him down with such force that he became insensible. For several moments he knew nothing of what happened,[1] but when he came to, he heard a shot and felt a pain in his thigh. What does he see too, but that he is in a tiger's jaws. Some one had fired at the tiger and hit him, but luckily the tiger had not injured him as yet, for only his clothes and pouch-belt were in its mouth. In short, the sepoy, somehow or other (*jūṅ tūṅ karke*), managed to get out his bayonet, and plunged it into the tiger's body. The tiger leapt aside and the sepoy was freed from its jaws, but the tiger returned at once and seized him again. The poor sepoy could now scarcely breathe, but such an opportunity now presented itself to him that he could deliver a mortal blow. He stabbed it violently several times behind the shoulder. The tiger staggered and fell and began to struggle (flutter) on the ground. The wounded sepoy now thought that he[2] was safe out of the clutches of his tyrant, and was just getting up, when the tiger gave a terrible roar and rose, and springing forward wanted to seize its prey but fell on its side, and turning over[3] reached the sepoy's feet, who at once thrust his bayonet into its heart (*lit.* liver).

In India and in other countries of Asia, too, there are several devices for catching tigers. Sometimes a deep pit is dug and covered over, so as to appear ordinary ground (*k͟hāṣī zamīn*). Sometimes in the path that a tiger habitually takes, a bow and poisoned arrows are so placed that when the tiger passes by, they come and strike it. Sometimes very heavy beams are so arranged that if a rope is just (*zarā*) touched by the tiger's foot, the beam falls. In the Madras Presidency the following device is resorted to: many men collect and surround

1 Note idiom.

2 Direct narration.

3 P*alṭā khānā* "to turn; *also* to rebound and to ricochet."

a tiger and drive it gradually into a net and snare it: they then despatch it with spears. In some places they put poison into the half-eaten 'kill' of a tiger, which it has temporarily left and to which it means to return.[1] When the tiger returns and feeds, the poison takes effect and it dies. Sometimes the following plan is resorted to (*ki*): Shikārīs sit in a tree or a *machān* over the fresh 'kill' of a cow or bullock left by a tiger;[1] or sometimes they themselves tie up a live bullock and when the tiger comes it is shot.

The Chinese catch the tiger by a strange device (*kal*).[2] They place a large box where the tiger passes to and fro, and to its side they fasten a mirror. The tiger seeing its reflection comes close to the chest, and, entering it, is at once trapped.

There is a country called Malākā where they employ a different method. They mix poison with a sticky substance like bird-lime and rub it on a number of broad leaves, and lay them in the track of the tiger. When it goes to that place and puts its feet on the leaves, one or two leaves stick to a paw. When it tries[3] to remove them with the other paw, the leaves stick the tighter to it. The tiger, getting irritated, rubs its paw on its face and the leaves then stick to its face too. Enraged, it begins to roll on the ground, and its whole body gets stuck over with the leaves; and when it scratches itself and rubs itself, some of the poisoned bird-lime gets into the eyes too, and blinds it. At last, unable to bear the pain, it roars. The shikārīs are hid in the neighbourhood, and as soon as they hear the noise of the roaring they are on the spot, and finish off the poor beast.

In the northern districts of India, the Sardars and English officers generally shoot tigers off elephants, but in Southern and Central India they generally shoot on foot, but this is very

[1] Note the order in the original sentence: translate it literally and learn by heart.

[2] What are the proper meanings of *kal*?

[3] *Chāhtā hai.*

risky. The following is the method of shooting from elephants. The elephants, formed in line, advance through the jungle, and when a tiger is seen, it is at once fired at. When a tiger is wounded, it usually becomes enraged and charges. Sometimes it comes on so threateningly (bullyingly), that the elephant shows it a clean pair of heels; but elephants trained to tiger-shooting stand firm. Some elephants charge the tiger of their own accord and try (*chāhte haiṅ*) to crush it with their knees, but this is very awkward for the people in the hauda (*haude ke sawār*) whose lives are sometimes endangered. Once an elephant evinced its bravery in this manner, and the ṣāḥib in the *hauda* fell forward, and his foot chanced to go straight into the tiger's jaws. The ṣāḥib was very quick; he left nothing except his shoe in the tiger's mouth, and dragged out his foot by force. Still he was lamed for life.

If a tiger is caught quite young and reared, it becomes tame,[1] but still there is danger. There was a tiger of this description in the Lahore Zoo. It was as playful as a kitten. It was so tame, that visitors used to stroke its head and it did nothing. Once it escaped from its cage. The Jamadar who was its keeper followed it and came near it, and folding his hands said, "Son, through you I earned my living; if you do not come back, I lose my bread. If you injure anyone, my life too will be in danger. Come along, come along." Saying this he cast his *pagṛī* round its neck and led it back to the Zoo. Though the tiger did not understand the words, still it must have known that[2] he was the same kind person who fed it daily and fondled it. One day a boy was standing with his hand in the cage of that self-same tiger. The tiger made one snap and wrenched off his hand and eat it up. The boy was lucky to get off with his life (*g͟hanīmat yih hai ki*).—After this even the boy used to come and visit the friend that had given him a keepsake.

[1] Why *hil-jātā hai* and not *hiltā hai*? What is the meaning of *hilā hūā*? *Vide* "Hindustani Stumbling-Blocks," IX, Supplement.

[2] Direct narration.

The people of India have several superstitions (*wahm*) regarding certain portions of the tiger's body; for instance, they fancy that if the whiskers are given to a person to eat, they will so pierce his entrails that he will die. In some parts of India the people entertain this belief, too, that if anyone keeps a tiger's whiskers by him, he becomes wonderfully strong. Some persons have a firm belief that if the claws of a tiger are bound on to the necks of children they protect them from the evil eye and evil spirits. Tiger's claws are encased in gold and silver and are considered to be amulets, and are worn as ornaments.

45. THE HYÆNA.

This animal too walks on the fore part of the feet. In the fore-paws of cats and dogs, etc., there are five toes and in the hind-paws four; but all four paws of this animal have four toes, and its claws too are not retractile like those of the cat and the tiger. Although in height it is not very much taller than a big dog, still the muscles of its chest and neck are very much stronger. It chews up hard bones with astonishing ease; it chews the thigh-bone of an ox with such ease that one must see it doing it to realize the fact. A great strain (*zor*) falls on the bones of its neck: the joints of its neck are so joined that its neck always remains stiff, and hence people fancy that it is composed of one bone only. Its hind legs are crooked. The hind parts, compared to the head and shoulders, are so small that one is astonished at its ungainly shape. It is on account of this shape that it has a rolling gait. Its voice is harsh (*kaṛā*) and unpleasing. Sometimes its cry is like that of a person laughing loudly.

This animal lives in *nālās*, or in holes and caves in the low hills. Though powerful in body, it is cowardly. By day it sleeps in its cave, and by night it comes out to hunt for food. It subsists on decayed carcasses. It even digs down and extracts dead bodies from the graves. Though it is a filthy and disgusting animal, still it is useful in many ways; for if it did not eat up carcasses the air would be polluted.

animal, it will stick to it and follow it for miles and remain watching it with great patience, eager in its mind[1] for it to become lifeless, so that it may devour it. When no meat of any kind is to be obtained, it manages to subsist (*guzārā karnā*) on roots and the young leaves of small palm-trees. When nothing is to be found, it becomes infuriated and dangerous,[2] and wanders round habitations seeking for strayed sheep. If it comes across a dog, it will devour it even. It attacks even women and children. The young can be easily tamed and show great affection for their master.

[1] *Ki wuh kab* ——— "saying that, 'When will ———.'"

[2] Note how this is expressed in the original.

46. THE BEAR.

This is a very ungainly animal, covered with long hair from head to foot; tiny ears, a long snout, long and strong claws fitted for digging. It is expert in climbing. In most species there is no hair on the sole of the foot. The bear places its feet on the ground and progresses like man, and its footprints have the same appearance as his. Between it and animals that walk on their toes[1] like the cat, dog, hyæna, etc., there is a great difference. The sole of the bear's foot is broad and flat, and hence it can somewhat easily erect itself on its hind legs. When attacked by an enemy, it rears up and confronts him and fights well. It seizes its enemy by its hands, and pressing him to its broad chest so hugs him that the helpless enemy (*bichārā*)[2] is squeezed[3] to death. Although the bear is included amongst the carnivorous animals, still most species feed principally on roots, grains, fruits, insects, and honey. By day, the bear hides in caves in hills, in hollow trees, and in bushes. At night, it comes out in search of food. Bears have a very strange habit: when sitting idle, especially after feed-

[1] Digitigrade.

[2] For *be-chāra*.

[3] *Ghutnā*, "to lose one's breath: be strangled."

ing, they suck and suck their paws "drumming"[1] the while. This sound can be heard from a great distance issuing out of caves and fissures in the hills.

There are several species of bears, but in India, three kinds are well known, the brown, and the black bear of the Himalayas, and another species of black bear found in other parts. If the young of any of these species is taken when very young, it is easily tamed. Bears are often trained, and made to dance, and taught many tricks (*kartab*), and are carried about the bazars to earn a living for their masters.

The brown bear of the Himalayas is the largest of these three species; it lives in high mountains on the verge of the snows. Grass and the roots of plants are its chief food. When the fruit-season comes it comes down into the jungles to eat fruit. It comes near cultivation too, and eats apples, walnuts and most kinds of fruit. It is also fond of insects, and turns over stones, searching for them. By winter, it has become very fat and lies up in some cave. The whole winter it remains there dozing: it doesn't want even to eat or drink. When winter is nearly over, it comes out again, and again begins to feed. Compared with the brown bear, the black bear of the Himalayas is very small. In the hot weather it remains high up in the hills and generally keeps near the snow-line, but in the winter, as the snow falls lower down, so it too comes down lower into the passes. It lives on various kinds of roots, grains, and fruit. To get at the fruit, it climbs trees. It is very fond of honey. The hill-people who keep bees, construct their hives in the walls of their huts, for the sake of protecting them; but the bear sometimes takes out the honey from them.[2] Sometimes, too, it kills sheep and goats; but usually

[1] *G͟hur g͟hur* غُر غُر, f. (*k.*), is generally the low noise in the throat of anger; growling. *K͟har k͟har*, خر خر f. (*k.*), is the noise of snoring or the death rattle. *Ghur ghur* گُھر گُھر is the purring of a cat. Note that all inarticulate sounds are feminine because *āwāz* is feminine; but such words as *shor* and *g͟hul*, etc., are of both genders.

[2] Note the force of *hī* in this clause.

it does not eat flesh. Its powers of vision are not great, but of course its powers of scent are acute. Should anyone approach its direction from up-wind (*hawā ke rukh se*), it becomes alert. If you attack it, it usually does nothing but run off; but if the way of escape is blocked, it will fiercely confront (its adversary). It generally strikes at a man's head in attack, and whips off (*uṛā-lenā*) his scalp, and so mutilates his face that he becomes a frightening object.

The second species of black bear is found in abundance in those places where there are low hills, and rocks, and caves. Such bears do a great deal of damage. Many are found in the Vindhiyāchal hills. They often attack wood-cutters. When any one pursues the female, she saves her young [1] by carrying it off on her back. This species of bear subsists on ants, white-ants, various small insects, honey, dates, and other fruits. Sometimes the bears harry birds' nests and eat the eggs. They have great powers of sucking in their breath. They dig up the abodes of the termites with their paws and blow away the earth, and then placing the snout on the hole, snuff up with such violence that the white-ants and their larvæ are drawn up from a distance.

The white bear is the largest of all. On the shores of the Arctic regions, far from here, snow is always on the ground, and in the sea too whole mountains of ice lie about every where, and for miles the water remains frozen: there these bears dwell. The soles of their feet are covered with thick hair, and hence they can run with ease on slippery ice. They swim in the water too, and dive. Sometimes they catch hares, and extract the young of birds from their nests and eat them, but their food is chiefly fish and seals [*lit.* 'sea-calf']. This last too is a strange animal that will be described later on.

[1] What is the meaning of, *Wuh bahut khānā chaṛhā-gayā hai*?

47. THE PALM-SQUIRREL.

This animal is wonderfully sportive and restless. One is delighted at the quickness of its movements. It is very impudent and artful; very fearless and mischievous. It sees a dog stalking it, but feigns ignorance (*an-jān bannā*); when the dog gets quite near, it runs off chattering; and, clinging to the trunk of a tree, climbs up it and keeps on looking back at its powerless enemy as though jeering at it.

When it squats [1] on its heels (*ukṛūṅ* [2] *baiṭhnā*) on a branch, holding some hard fruit in its tiny paws, it gnaws off the outer peel with its long sharp teeth in a manner surprising to see. Pick up a fruit or a grain gnawed (*kutarnā*) by it, and see how the marks of its teeth are left. Do you remember what was said about the hare? This animal too, like the hare and the rat and the mouse, is a rodent. However hard the substance may be, it is seldom that it cannot be penetrated by its sharp chisel-like teeth.

You will certainly say that, "If the squirrel and other rodents are always working their teeth, and are always gnawing all kinds of hard substances, their teeth must get worn down and blunted. The carpenter sharpens his chisel and the shoemaker his awl, and all instruments with sharp edges by continnal wear (*ghisnā*) become blunt; but the squirrel never sharpens its teeth." It's true (*hāṅ*) it doesn't sharpen them, but God has made its teeth in a cunning manner. The outside surface (*ru<u>kh</u>*) is very hard, and wears down very slowly; but the inside is soft, and as it gets worn, the teeth become slanting, and the outside remains sharp. When you mend an Indian reed-pen, see, you pare it on one side only, and the other side grows sharp and thin. Again you will say, "The teeth will gradually get shorter and shorter by wear." Certainly this would ordinarily be the case; but the teeth of rodents continue to grow as long as the animal lives: [3] whereas the teeth of other animals grow at once to the size they have to attain.

The squirrel lives chiefly in trees. It makes its nest of grass,

[1] Note that in the original both verbs are habitual.

[2] *Vide* under the article on the Mongoose for another expression.

[3] Note the order of this clause in Hindustani.

thatch, or in the beams of the roof. It lives on buds, kernels, and fruit. Frequently, too, it comes into the houses for bits of bread, and seeds. In search of food, it descends to the ground and then (now) birds of prey sometimes pounce on (*jhapaṭnā*) it, and carry it off. Small children catch the young and tame them, feeding them on milk.

48. THE MUSK-RAT.

Just listen! What is this squealing noise? There must be some animal behind the ward-robe. Just make a noise with your stick and frighten it away. Look! look! there it is running off. Uff, uff! What a nasty smell there is. This is a musk-rat. Don't call the cat; it won't kill it. The cat kills mice and rats but it feels a disgust at the evil-smell of this animal. It is by [1] this very smell that this weak and cowardly animal protects itself. If you have ever examined it attentively, you must have discovered how conical and long its snout is. This snout at once proclaims the fact (*kah-denā*) that it is not a rat. Its front teeth too are not like those of rodents. On its grinders (*ḍāṛh*, f.) there are small sharp projections (*khār*). These animals grind whatever they eat; for this reason God has given them flat grinders. You recollect—you read it in the 3rd Part—that the musk-rat is an insect-eating animal like the field-rat. Its sharp-pointed teeth are useful for preying on insects. The feet of the musk-rat are small and fine, and it also progresses after the manner of insect-eating animals like the bear. It does not walk on the fore-part of its feet like the dog, the cat, and the hyæna. On both its sides, under the skin, are glands, and it is from them that the scent issues. There is a smell like musk in its scent, but stinking and unpleasing. This scent has a peculiar property; anything over which a musk-rat once passes becomes pervaded with its smell. If

1 ———— *kī ba-daulat.*

it runs over any vessel of water, the water becomes so stinking that it can't be drunk, and fastidious people can't support the smell even from a distance. What is more, it is commonly said that if a bottle is closed with a cork and a musk-rat runs over it, then the contents of the bottle too become stinking. If flour or any other eatable is touched by it, the stench remains for a long time.

Its colour is very like that of the earth (*maṭyālā sā*), but the tips (*nok*) of the hairs are a little inclined to red, and their colour can be distinctly perceived in a bright light. The musk-rat is found in hot countries ; cold is very trying to it. You must have noticed that it is rarely heard in the cold weather. As the heat increases, this animal is found more and more in houses. By day, it hides in drains, holes [*bil*, hole of an animal], in dark closets, or underneath boxes and matting ; but at night it comes out to hunt. It is useful too, in a way, for it preys on crickets, dung-beetles, mosquitoes, and other insects.

ENGLISH TRANSLATION
OF
THE VAZIR OF LANKURAN:

A PLAY IN FOUR ACTS, TRANSLATED FROM PERSIAN INTO URDU AND EDITED WITH COPIOUS NOTES.

BY

SHAMS-UL-'ULAMĀ MAULAVI MUḤAMMAD YUSUF JA'FARI, KHAN BAHADUR,
Head Maulavi, Board of Examiners,

AND

LIEUT.-COLONEL D. C. PHILLOTT, F.A.S.B.,
Secretary and Member, Board of Examiners;
Fellow of the Calcutta University.

CALCUTTA:

PRINTED AT THE BAPTIST MISSION PRESS.

1911.

THE VAZIR OF LANKURAN.

DRAMATIS PERSONÆ.

Mirzā Ḥabīb ..	.. The Wazīr of the Khān of Lankurān.
Ḥaidar	.. The Wazīr's Farrāsh.
Karīm	.. The Wazīr's Groom.
Āqā Bashīr ..	.. The Wazīr's Steward.
Farrāshes of the Wazīr	.. Several individuals.
Zebā Khānum ..	.. The Wazīr's chief wife.
Shu'la Khānum ..	.. The Wazīr's young and favourite wife, Nisā Khānum's elder sister.
Nisā Khānum ..	.. The Wazīr's sister-in-law, Tīmūr Āqā's sweetheart.
Parī Khānum ..	.. The Wazīr's mother-in-law, who, with her younger daughter, Nisā Khānum, is staying in the Wazīr's residence.
Āqā Mas'ūd Ḥabshī	.. The Wazīr's Eunuch, *i.e.*, Chamberlain of the women's apartments.
The Khān	.. Governor of Lankurān.
'Azīz Āqā	.. The Khān's head-servant.
Salīm Beg	.. Master of the Ceremonies to the Khān.
Qadīr Beg	.. The Deputy Master of the Ceremonies.
Ṣamad Beg ..	.. The Chief of the Khān's Farrāshes.

Petitioners, Plaintiffs and Defendants.	Four individuals.
Farrāshes of the Khān ..	Several individuals.
Officials and Nobles of the Province.	Several individuals.
Guards ..	Fifty men.
Tīmūr Āqā	The nephew of the Khān of Lankurān, Nisā Khānum's lover.
Rizā ..	Foster-brother of Tīmūr Āqā.
Hājī Sālih ..	A Merchant.
A Doctor .	

ACT I.

[The scene is laid at the town of Lankurān, on the shores of the Caspian, some fifty years ago, in the house of Mirzā Ḥabīb, the Wazīr. The Wazīr is seated in a room at the entrance of his harem, and Ḥājī Ṣāliḥ is standing before him.]

Wazīr: Ḥājī Ṣāliḥ, I have heard you are going to Rasht.[1] Is that so?

Ḥājī Ṣāliḥ: Yes, sir; I am going there.

Wazīr: Ḥājī Ṣāliḥ, I have a commission for you. You must carry it out for me. This was why I sent for you.

Ḥājī Ṣāliḥ: Be pleased to command me, sir. I am ready, heart and soul, to carry out the orders of Your Excellency.

Wazīr: Well Ḥājī, you must get a blue, gold-embroidered jacket made in Rasht; but remember no one must ever have been its like in Lankurān. When the jacket is ready, you must get a goldsmith to make twenty-four gold buttons, smaller than a hen's egg, bigger than a pigeon's. Have them sewn round the collar of the jacket. When you return, bring it with you. Here, take these fifty pieces of gold.

[He puts the coins, wrapped up in paper, before Ḥājī Ṣāliḥ.]

Pay for everything, and if the money is short, I will settle with you on your return here. You are coming back soon—aren't you?

Ḥājī Ṣāliḥ: In another month I shall be back; I have no important business to do. I am taking ready money to buy silk and then return. But, sir, if you gave me the size of the jacket now, it would be as well. The tailor in Rasht may make it too tight or too loose, or too long or too short, and then Your Excellency will find fault with me.

Wazīr: It does not matter. If they make it a little too tight or too loose, well let them. It can be put right here.

[1] Rasht, in Gīlān. It is on the southern shore of the Caspian Sea It is famous for its embroidery.

Ḥājī Ṣāliḥ: Will it not do, sir, if I buy the cloth, and have the buttons made, and bring them all here? The coat can then be cut and made to the Khānum's figure.

Wazīr: Oh, you men! you have a curious habit of talking and making a display of your wisdom. Your intention is that I should tell you openly about my private affairs. Don't you know that if I give the jacket to be cut out and made up here, how much it will be talked about and how I shall be pestered with questions?

Ḥājī Ṣāliḥ: No, sir, how should I know anything about it?

Wazīr: Well, I must acquaint you with the matter lest when you go to the bazar, you tell some one that the Wazīr has entrusted you with such and such a service, and the matter gets abroad, and then I shan't have any peace, or be allowed to sit down a moment in quiet. My dear friend, the matter is this; in two months it will be New Year's Day,[1] and on that occasion I must make Shu'la Khānum a little present.[2] If the coat is made here, Zebā Khānum too will naturally persist in demanding one like it. If I give her one, it's mere waste of money. How in the name of the Devil will a coat like *this* suit a woman like *that*?——and if I don't give her one, when shall I be free from her chatter and nagging? It will be every day disturbance, every day quarrelling. Who would not fight shy of that?

Ḥājī Ṣāliḥ: But, sir, when you give the jacket to Shu'la Khānum, won't Zebā Khānum too see it, and then demand to be given one just like it?

Wazīr: Oh Allah, what I have to put up with! O creature of God,[3] what business is that of yours? Carry out your orders. Listen; when I give the jacket to Shu'la Khānum I will make out that my sister, the wife of Hidāyat Khān of Rasht, has sent it as a little present to Shu'la Khānum; then Zebā Khānum won't be able to accuse me of carelessness, or neglect. But have

1 *Naw Roz*, the Persian New Year's Day, the 21st of March. It is *the* festival of the year. Everyone expects a present.

2 *Tuḥfa*, any rarity or curiosity.

3 *Mard-i Khudā* and sometimes also *mard-i ādmī*.

a care ; on no account repeat to any one a single word of what I've told you.

Ḥājī Ṣāliḥ: God forbid ; what good do I get by blabbing ? Would such a thing be worthy of me ?

Wazīr: Well,—good-bye : you may go ; now let me see you on the move.

[Ḥājī Ṣāliḥ makes his obeisance and goes out. The moment he is out of the room, Zebā Khānum bursts open the opposite door with both hands and rushes in, making a great uproar. The Wazīr, startled by the noise, looks behind him in alarm.]

Zebā Khānum: Well sir ! So you were giving an order for a gold-buttoned, embroidered jacket for your darling of a wife ? May I be sacrificed for this sort of generosity of yours. Oh yes ! and you would tell me that your "sister, the wife of Hidāyat Khān of Rasht, has sent it as a little present to Shu'la Khānum ?" Glory to God ! So you are starting to teach me what your sister is like !—Your sister who's such a skin-flint that like the traders of Iṣfahān she shuts up a bit of cheese in a bottle and then rubs her bread on the outside of the glass before eating it.[1] And does she now so overflow with generosity that she sends a jacket worth fifty or sixty tumāns as a little present to that darling wife of yours ? Have I become such a complete ass that I should have believed you ?

Wazīr: Old woman ! You frighten me. You are saying—what ? what jacket ? Has your brain turned ?

Zebā Khānum: Now stop inventing—no pretences if you please. All that you were saying to Ḥājī Ṣāliḥ, I heard it all, every word, every letter, from the beginning right up to the end. The moment you sent for Ḥājī Ṣāliḥ, I knew at once what you were after—my mind was filled with doubt. I came on tiptoe and stood behind that very door. I heard all. I learnt that my suspicions were true to the letter. Now may God make that gold-buttoned embroidered jacket auspicious for your beloved darling. Won't Tīmūr Āqā's eyes sparkle ? Let us

[1] A form of "potatos and point."

say, "An order has been issued for a jacket for *his* sweetheart." She will put it on, and peacock-like, will strut, and dance, and posture before him.

Wazīr: What rubbish are you chattering, old woman? Will you never stop your incoherencies? Have you no shame? Such a calumny against my consort, and in my presence? You dishonour me. In this world modesty counts for *something*, but I'm sorry it has not even touched *you*.

Zebā Khānum: All right. Had I wished to dishonour you, wouldn't I have made love to one of these fascinating and smart young fellows? It's your beloved darling of a wife who throws your honour to the winds, who for the whole twenty-four hours keeps Tīmūr Āqā close by her side. My maid has seen her often and often like this, with her own eyes.

Wazīr [turning pale]: I don't believe you and I don't believe your maid.

Zebā Khānum: It isn't *we* only who say this. Who is there in Lankurān who doesn't know all about it? Everybody says that you have shut your eyes like a *chakor*[1] and think nobody can see. A blind man thinks all the rest of the world blind. You can't see what's good and bad for you and think the rest of the world can't either.

Wazīr: What are you talking about? What does Shu'la Khānum know of Tīmūr Āqā? When has she ever seen him?

Zebā Khānum: You yourself pointed him out to her. You yourself showed him to her.

Wazīr [raising his voice]: *I* showed him to her? *I* pointed him out to her?

Zebā Khānum: Yes, yes. *You*[2] pointed him out to her. If you didn't, who did—*I*? Now didn't you come on the *'Īd* festival and tell your darling that by the Khān's orders the

[1] *i.e.*, like an ostrich sticking its head in the sand. "To shut the eyes like a *chakor* and stick one's head under the snow" is a Persian idiom.

[2] Note that the emphatic-*hīñ* equals italics; *vide* "Hindustani Manual," page 182 (*e*), and "Hindustani Stumbling-Blocks," VIII, 15.

young gentlemen of the place were going to have wrestling matches outside the fort, and didn't you tell her and Nisā Khānum to come with their maids and their eunuch and spread a rug and sit there and watch the show? Well they all went there, and Tīmūr Āqā, a fascinating, smart, good-looking fellow, threw all the young nobles. As soon as Shu'la Khānum saw him, she fell madly in love with him. Who knows by what devices she has ensnared him in her love? Matters have now reached such a pitch with Shu'la that if she misses seeing him *one* day she begins to flutter like a dying chicken. Why—didn't I tell you from the very first that it was most improper for an old person like you, at such an age as yours, to marry a skittish young filly? But when did you ever listen to me? Now—well, it serves you right.

Wazīr: All right, all right, that's quite enough; stop your quacking: leave me alone; get out; go to Hell; I have some business to do.

Zebā Khānum [going out muttering]: "Why should *I* go to Hell? To Hell with your darling and her paramour. It's proper for a man like you to have to do with persons of that sort."

Wazīr [to himself]: I *cannot* believe that Shu'la Khānum can have done such a thing. Of course (*hān*) it is possible she may have admired Tīmūr Āqā's strength and pluck,—and then the simple child may have thoughtlessly praised him to a few people, and so this old woman, through envy and spite (*ḥasad*), may have cast this calumny at her, wishing to dig a pitfall for her. Well, whatever may be the case, I must put the idea out of Shu'la's mind. Somehow or other I must impress upon her that Tīmūr Āqā is not really as strong as she thinks he is. I will say—"After all, who were those whom Tīmūr Āqā threw? They were mere boys." By this means I will lessen Tīmūr Āqā's importance, and she will put him out of mind, and not even let his name cross her lips again. Now I must go to the Khān. On my return I will visit Shu'la Khānum and see what I can do.

[He gets up to go.]

Zebā Khānum [enters]: Please inform me what you would like for breakfast[1] and dinner to-day, so that I may have it cooked for you.

Wazīr: Enough, enough! Your abuse and reproaches have filled me to satiety, and I don't expect to feel hungry again for a month. [He begins to go. There is a sieve lying on the floor. Lost in thought, his eyes on the door, he goes straight on, putting his foot on the edge of the sieve which flies up and catches him a rap on the knee. He sits down with a wry face and hugs his knee, and screams to his wife.] Ah—I'm killed! What is this sieve lying here for? What rascals! Curse them.

Zebā Khānum [in astonishment]: What do *I* know about it? How can *I* tell why this sieve is lying here? Whenever you honour this place with your presence, you bring a basket-load of 'nice words' too, for me. Some one else may wear the jacket, but *I* must listen to the abuse!

Wazīr: Farrāsh!

[Ḥaidar the farrāsh enters, folds his arms, and bows. Zebā Khānum veils her face and retires into a corner.]

Wazīr [getting into a rage]: Ḥaidar! this sieve—why is it lying in the middle of the room?

Ḥaidar: Ḥuẓūr! I was sweeping the room[2] this morning, when Karīm the sais came in with a sieve in his hand. He said something to me and went away. It seems that he left the sieve here when he went out.

Wazīr: Call that bastard of a sais here—I'll see to him. [The farrāsh goes out to summon the sais.] Good God![3] What business has a sais in my *room*, and what is a sieve doing in my *room*? I can't imagine whose face I saw when I got up this morning[4] that I meet with nothing but disaster.

1 The Persian *déjeuner* or *nahār* is taken at noon.

2 There are no *mihtars* in Persia.

3 *Subḥānaʾ 'llah*, lit. "Holiness to God."

4 Certain faces are lucky and certain unlucky. Some Persians make a servant with a lucky face sleep near, so that his may be the first face seen in the morning.

Whenever I come into this infernal room I meet with some mischance or other.

Zebā Khānum: Of course, and why not—seeing that Shu'la Khānum is not here. Such being the case why do you ever come here at all? Kindly honour *her* room only in future.

[The farrāsh and the sais enter.]

Wazīr [beside himself with rage]: Karīm, you brat![1] Why did you come into my room? Your place is the stable. How dare you set foot inside my room? You, bastard, you![2]

Sais: Gharīb-parwar! I came here for a moment just to ask[3] if Your Honour would ride to-day. I asked and went out again immediately.

Wazīr: But why did you leave the sieve behind you?

Sais: I had the sieve in my hand to clean the horses' barley, and left it here by mistake (*bhūlkar*).

Wazīr: Then why didn't you come back for it?

Sais: I had no idea I had left it here. I have been hunting for it (*talāsh kartā phirtā thā*) everywhere, ever since.

Wazīr [first addressing the sais and then the farrāsh]: What were you thinking of, you, rascal, you (—*kahīṅ kā*)? Ḥaidar! Call Āqā Bashīr, the steward; call him quickly,—and bring too the pole and switches with you.[4] [The farrāsh goes out.]

Sais [trembling violently and weeping as he speaks]: For the sake of God and His Prophet, forgive me!

Wazīr [restraining his anger, and in a soft voice]: Hold your tongue, you son of a pig!

Sais [whimperingly]: May I be your sacrifice! I have erred—I have repented. Forgive me as a sacrifice on your dear father's tomb; please. I have committed a fault. Every hair

1 *Launḍā* is always contemptuous.

2 Notice this idiomatic use of *kahīṅ* fellow, or creature: *vide* "Hindustani Stumbling-Blocks."

3 Direct narration.

4 *Falak* or *falaka* is the bastinado-pole: it has a noose in the middle for the feet. Two farrāshes, one at each end, support the pole so that the culprit's feet are held with the soles towards the sky.

of my body has sinned against you. I will never again set foot in this room.

Wazīr: Curse you![1] you, bastard-spawn, you!

[The steward Āqā Bashīr, and Ḥaidar the farrāsh carrying a bundle of withes under his arm, enter with three other farrāshes; all bow.]

Wazīr [addressing the farrāshes]: Throw the steward and fasten his feet to the pole.

[The farrāshes throw the steward and fasten his feet in the noose. One hither and one thither, hold the pole, and two pick up the withes.]

Wazīr: Beat. [The farrāshes beat.]

Steward: Oh, oh! I'm killed quite! May I be your sacrifice! What is my fault? Oh why are they beating me?

Wazīr [pointing angrily]: Why is this sieve lying in the middle of my room?

Steward: Ḥuẓūr! What sort of sieve?

Wazīr: When you've been beaten you'll know what sort of sieve. [The farrāshes begin to beat again.]

Steward: Pity, pity! Justice, justice! May I be your sacrifice! Please, only tell me what my fault is. May I be your sacrifice! For God's sake tell me my fault. Then if you like kill me outright—you are at liberty to kill me.

Wazīr [addressing the farrāshes]: Rest a little. Āqā Bashīr, your fault is this; you have not taught the out-door servants their duty. It is *your* duty to make the outside servants work. It is *your* business to explain to each one *what* his work is and *where* it is. It is not the *sais's* business to set his foot outside the stable. Recollect that sieves are not to be left in my room. Karīm came to-day into my room and left his sieve behind him. My foot happened to fall on its edge and the other edge flew up and caught me a whack on the knee. The blow was so violent that I can't even yet move my leg. *I* manage a whole Province and *you*—ass, fool,—can't you even keep one house and its servants in order?

1 Lit. "may you be robbed," and hence = "ruined."

Steward: Oh noble sir! what am I to be compared to you? Your Honour is the Plato of this age: how on earth can *I* vie with you?

Wazīr [to farrāshes]: Beat, beat.

Steward: May I be Your Honour's sacrifice! Forgive me this once. Never again will your slave commit such a fault.

Wazīr: Very well, stop. Now that he has promised, well and good; let him go. Enough punishment for this time. Āqā Bashīr! I[1] forgive you this time. But if a sieve is again found in my room, look out, for it will be the worse for you.—Hāh!

Steward [getting up]: Rest assured of that.

Wazīr: Go, go; go away.

Sais [aside]: God, I thank Thee!

[The curtain falls.]

[1] *Kartā hūn=Main ne qūṣūr mu'āf kiyā.*

ACT II.

[Takes place in Shu'la K͟hānum's Room.]

Tīmūr Āqā [standing facing Nisā K͟hānum]: Tell me what I should do? What disorder[2] is this that has taken possession of the Wazīr's brain? Am I then dead that he wants to marry you to some one else? What good will it do him to get himself related to the K͟hān?

Nisā K͟hānum: What, don't you know what his object is? His object is power, honour, dignity.[3]

Tīmūr Āqā: But are not the power, and honour, and dignity, he now has from the K͟hān sufficient for him?

Nisā K͟hānum: Oh yes, they are enough for him, but what dependence is there on them? He wants to bring about the relationship with this end, that his power and dignity, etc., may be made lasting.

Tīmūr Āqā: He is a strangely foolish person. From what you say (*is se*) one would suppose that he had not seen with his

[2] *K͟habṭ* "disorder, disarrangement'" (not madness).

[3] *Izzat*, gen., honour. *Ḥurmat*, honour and also chastity

own eyes all the things (*kyā kyā*) the Ḵẖān has done to his other relations. Well, whatever may be the reason, we must exert ourselves to get our business settled as *we* want it. It is for nothing that you have so long stopped me from mentioning this matter to him. To-morrow I will send him an oral message by some one and inform him of everything, so that he may give up his foolish projects. If he won't, it won't go well with him.

Nisā Ḵẖānum : For God's sake, sir, give up this intention of yours—it is not possible to mention the matter to the Wazīr : he has been remarking for some time (*kab se*) that the Ḵẖān is ever seeking for some excuse (pretence) to kill you.[1] I know, too, that he has often consulted the Wazīr about doing so. If the Wazīr learns of our great [2] attachment, for his own ends he will go straight to the Ḵẖān and say, " Tīmūr Āqā is carrying on an intrigue with your intended." He is all the more likely to do this as the Ḵẖān is angry with you.

Tīmūr Āqā : The Ḵẖān has deprived me of my rights : he has usurped my father's throne (*gaddī* hereditary cushion). Is not this enough for the Ḵẖān, that he wants my life too ?

Nisā Ḵẖāuum : Of course he looks on you as a thorn in his side. I have often heard that he is in dread of your claiming your father's territory. He is obliged to treat you with kindness and courtesy before people ; but if—God forbid—he gets an opportunity, he won't let you live a day, not he.

Tīmūr Āqā : Ḵẖāns [3] like him can never take *my* life. Most of the people (*ri'āyā*) and all the nobles have a sincere attachment to me on account of my late [4] father. I'm no rat to be afraid of his mewing. But tell me what harm (*quṣūr*) have I ever done to the Wazīr that he should be annoyed with me ?

Nisā Ḵẖānum : You have made Mirzā Salīm, the son of the former Wazīr, your Secretary ; and the Wazīr thinks that if

---

[1] Lit. " Tīmūr Āqā ;" direct narration.

[2] *Ishq o muḥabbat* ; note synonymous words to indicate excess.

[3] " A Ḵẖān like him " would be, *is jaisā—*

[4] Why *marḥūm* ? How do Hindus express ' late ' ?

you get into power you will put Mirzā Salīm into his father's old place: so he now wants to induce the Khān to banish Mirzā Salīm.

Tīmūr Āqā: My Secretary is not to be banished at his bidding. Such ideas with regard to *me*? May—God grant it—my father's salt that he has eaten, come out in leprous spots on his body! Please God all his plans will come to naught [1] and I will at last [2] attain my end. But of course (*hāṅ*) you are right to say that the Wazīr must not learn of our mutual (*bāhamī*) attachment. Where is Shu'la Khānum? I have something to say to her.

Nisā Khānum: She is with darling mother.

Tīmūr Āqā: Can't you go and call them here?

Nisā Khānum: Darling mother does not live in this house. Let us both go to *her*.

Tīmūr Āqā: All right, come along. We'll both go.

(EXIT BOTH. A LITTLE LATER—)

Zebā Khānum [entering quickly]: You, prostitute, you (*kahiṅ kī*)! Have you become so bold that you abuse my maid and make her worry my life out with her screaming and crying? Has the Wazīr turned your head so much? [She now notices that the room is empty; she looks all about.] Ah! where has the whore gone? May God wipe out the house of the Wazīr who has brought such evil days upon me. [She is just on the point of going out [3] when she hears a man's voice, and getting very frightened sits down.] Oh, oh, this is the voice of some strange man! Oh, oh, he's going to come in here! Oh Allah, what shall I do? I can't go out. Oh! oh— where shall I annihilate myself?

[She goes all round the room and at last goes behind the *parda*. Tīmūr Āqā and Shu'la Khānum enter.]

Tīmūr Āqā: How quickly your mother returned from the

[1] Note this idiom.

[2] Note how 'at last' is expressed; *vide* "Hindustani Manual," page 86, end of (*b*).

[3] Note how this is expressed in Hindustani.

baths! We had no time at all to chat in her room and I had many things to say to you. I hope the Wazīr won't [1] come into this room?

Shu'la Khānum: Set your mind at ease; the Wazīr can't come to these apartments to-day.

Tīmūr Āqā: Why can't he?

Shu'la Khānum: Because to-day it is Zebā Khānum's turn. Do you suppose he would dare to come here to-day and face Zebā Khānum's brawling and abuse?[2]

Tīmūr Āqā: That's all very well but how can one trust to that? One should still be cautious. He *might* enter suddenly.[3]

Shu'la Khānum: Don't be frightened. I have told Nisā Khānum to sit in the hall and not to leave it,[4] and that if she sees the Wazīr coming she is to come at once and warn us. What, are you afraid?

Tīmūr Āqā: No; why should[5] I be afraid? Of whom should I be afraid? I am not one of those who fear. But for several reasons I don't want the Wazīr to see me here and to go and tell the Khān. Before he has an opportunity to do that, there are several plans that I must carry out.

Shu'la Khānum: Of course,—the matter must not be known to the Wazīr, otherwise he would tell the Khān and then the secret would be out indeed.

Nisā Khānum: [Nisā Khānum now puts her head in at the door and cries]—

God save us, the Wazīr!

Shu'la Khānum [getting flurried and going to the door cries out]: Allah be our refuge! why (*to*) the Wazīr is coming straight towards *my* door. Ay, hay! Tīmūr Āqā, you can't manage to stay and you can't manage to go.

[1] Note this signification of *kahīṅ*; *vide* "Hindustani Sumbling-Blocks."

[2] What is the literal meaning of *salawāt*?

[3] What is the force of *paṛnā* in compounds?

[4] Note the force of *rahnā* in this compound.

[5] Note this use of *lagnā*; *vide* "Hindustani Stumbling-Blocks," XXII, 4.

Tīmūr Āqā: Then (*to*) what must I do? Perhaps some one has told him of my being here. If any one *has* told him of my being here, I swear by God I'll cut him in pieces with this knife of mine, and feed the kites and crows, and then [1] you'll see.

[He places his hand on his knife.]

Shu'la Khānum: This is not the time to talk; go behind that *parda*; hide. By some pretext or other I'll get rid of him.

[Tīmūr Āqā quickly goes behind the *parda*.]

Wazīr [enters limping]: Shu'la Khānum! what are you doing? I hope you're well?

Shu'la Khānum: Thanks to God! Through your prayers my health is always good. Kindly tell me how you are. It's a *very* unusual thing for you to have come here to-day. And why do you limp so? Why are you frowning? Every thing is all right —is it not?

Wazīr: Ugh! Such a thing has happened—don't ask me about it. I never even dreamt of such a thing. May God never punish my enemy even in such a manner. Āqā Mas'ūd! go and get me a cup of coffee.

[Āqā Mas'ūd makes an obeisance and goes out.]

Shu'la Khānum: Please sit down. Now just tell me what has happened, but no, no; it would take too long and would only be a worry to you.

Wazīr: No, it won't take long. The fact is I was sitting in the presence of the Khān with the other nobles when the subject of Tīmūr Āqā's strength cropped up. Everybody began to say that in all Lankurān there was no one who could match him in strength. The Khān too dittoed this, but I denied it. I said, "Although Tīmūr Āqā won several wrestling contests at the '*Īd*, still I don't admit his superior strength, because his opponents [2] were mere boys." Tīmūr Āqā too was there. The Khān didn't agree and asked me to prove it. I said, "It's not befitting my dignity; were it so (*warna*), then

[1] For the emphatic particle *sahī*, *vide* "Hindustani Manual," pages 202 (*d*), and 204-5.

[2] *Ḥarīf*.

in spite of my fifty years I would wrestle with him and you would see how I would throw him." The Khān, you know (*to*), is very fond of witnessing feats of gymnastics; he ordered me to wrestle with Tīmūr Āqā on the spot. I was powerless, so I got up. Tīmūr Āqā too got ready and faced me. Then, what was there to wait for? We shook hands, and then we actually closed. I was seized with emulation. Not a minute elapsed before I tripped him [1] and laid him out flat on the broad of his back I did not even know *how* I had thrown him; but when I looked, I saw the poor fellow lying senseless on his back. In somewhat less than half an hour he came to. The sudden effort I made when throwing him, strained my back (loins). It pains me still very much and I can't walk erect.

Shu'la Khānum [laughing out loud]: O crown of my head, what *have* you done? Supposing the poor fellow had died, what would his poor mother have done?

Wazīr: Of course, of course. I too was sorry afterwards. But what is the use of regretting now? What *was* to be, happened.

Shu'la Khānum: So the poor fellow was left lying there—and you came away here to tell me of your skill?

Wazīr: Oh no. The farrāshes dragged him off to his mother's house.

[Hearing this Tīmūr Āqā can't smother his laughter. The Wazīr jumps up, lifts up the *parda* and sees Tīmūr Āqā with Zebā Khānum, and stands dumb with amazement. Shu'la Khānum too is astonished at seeing Zebā Khānūm.]

Wazīr: My God! What strange thing is this! [Addressing Tīmūr Āqā in a shriek] Sir! what are you doing here? [Tīmūr Āqā hangs his head. The Wazīr again]. Well, at least, open your mouth; shake your head; loosen your tongue. You here, and why? What is your business here?

[Tīmūr Āqā makes no reply. He comes out from behind the *parda* and with a hang-dog look tries to make off.]

[1] *Langī* is any throw with the leg.

Wazīr [catching hold of his arm]: Do you think I'll let you go till you tell me what you were doing here? Speak, open your mouth, move your lips.

Tīmūr Āqā [jerking his arm]: Let go, let go.

Wazīr [holding all the tighter]: I won't let you go till you answer me.

[Tīmūr Āqā, finding himself in a corner, seizes hold of the Wazīr's collar by one hand and his legs by the other, and lifting him up casts him like a bundle of clothes into the middle of the room, and then springs off through the door.]

Wazīr [after a moment, pulling himself together sits up, and addresses Zebā K͟hānum]: You light-skirt! What disaster have you not dashed on my head?

Zebā K͟hānum: I dashed disaster on your head? What have *I* to do with the matter? You fool—who has told you this?

Wazīr [getting in a rage]: Shut your mouth, you whore, you, —don't quack. Oh, I've found you out. All these calumnies about others were just your own goings-on. Just see, I'll take care of you.

Zebā K͟hānum: Poor helpless creature! Well now, just tell me why you should take care of me. Have I acted against the law of the Prophet? have I taken a paramour? have I run away with another man? committed theft? disgraced my name? *what* have I done?

Wazīr: Bitch! Carrion! What more could you have done than hide behind a *parda* with a lusty young fellow?

Zebā K͟hānum: Squab of an owl! Just ask your darling Shu'la K͟hānum what business a strange man had in this room.

Wazīr: Trollop! First tell me what you were doing behind that *parda* with a strange [1] man.

Zebā K͟hānum: Very well. First *I'll* tell you, and then *she* will have her say. Let me see what she *will* say. Your beloved Shu'la K͟hānum called my maid some nasty names. I came to ask her why she didn't keep herself within bounds. My maid doesn't eat *her* salt. What right had she to call *my* maid

[1] *Nā-maḥram.*

names? When I came, I couldn't see any trace of her. I was just about to return when lo and behold Shu'la K͟hānum comes along joking and laughing with some man. I lost my head,—I couldn't go out, so I went behind the *parda* just to see what they were about, so that I could tell you all about them. As I hadn't my veil on, I couldn't stand before a *nā-maḥram*. It chanced that you came. When you drew near, *he* too had no help for it but to hide behind the *parda* till such time as you might go away.

Wazīr: If you're telling the truth, why didn't you come out from behind the *parda* that very instant?

Zebā K͟hānum: Do you suppose that I *could* come out? He threatened that if I uttered a sound he would finish me off with his dagger.

Wazīr [reflects a little and then addresses Shu'la K͟hānum]: Shu'la K͟hānum! tell me the whole truth. Did this man come to see you?

Shu'la K͟hānum: This wife of yours is a nightingale of a thousand notes. In fabricating tales and weaving tissues of falsehood she is just perfection. I have never even heard of the fellow nor do I know him by sight.

Wazīr: What! you have never heard of Tīmūr Āqā, you don't know him by sight? You know him very well by sight.

Shu'la K͟hānum: But how could Tīmūr Āqā come here? Didn't you throw him and send him off to his mother's house?

Wazīr: Faugh! What rubbish you are talking! Answer me. From what you say it is clearly evident that Tīmūr Āqā had come to you.

Shu'la K͟hānum: Oh no, *pardon* my impertinence. Had Tīmūr Āqā come to see *me*, you would have found him with *me*. Zebā K͟hānum knew that I would go to the baths to-day. Knowing that my room would be empty, it occurred to her that she could bring her lover here and make merry with him. She knew that to-day was the turn for Your Honour to visit *her* room, so she couldn't take him there. It chanced that there was no water in the baths to-day, so I came back. As I came in suddenly, they had no opportunity of going out; they hid behind the *parda*. They must have been enjoying themselves there, while waiting for an opportunity to get away when I went out. If you want the truth this is it. Pull yourself together and don't be deceived by the words of this shameless creature. Don't get suspicious of me without any reason.

Zebā Khānum [shrieking out at Shu'la Khānum]: Wretch! what lies you are concocting! You are putting your own crimes[1] on to me. Oh God, what shall I do? I'll kill myself!

Shu'la Khānum: It's you who are the wretch—you the whore. If you want to kill yourself, kill yourself; what do I care? There can't be such another tricky trollop as you in the whole of Lankurān. By screaming and crying you can't make yourself out to be chaste, and a gentlewoman. Your husband has eyes in his head. He can see for himself whether this business is my doing or yours.

Zebā Khānum: Pity, pity! Justice, justice! Oh God, in Thy hands is justice! I will kill myself! You, sir, why don't you give this whore a good hard slap for casting such calumnies at me? But you too stand there doing nothing but looking on.[2]

Shu'la Khānum: You harlot! why *should*[3] he slap me? If he were a man he would (must) cut you up into little bits. Were *you* caught with a strange man or was I?

Wazīr [addressing Zebā Khānum]: There is no doubt about it that you must be cut up into little bits. But just give me time (*muhlat*) to go to the Khān and first settle the business of your lover; then I'll look after you. You've spent the whole of your life telling lies—I know you well.

Zebā Khānum [getting into a rage]: Of course; I'm the only liar, while all of you, clad in the raiment of truth, came

1 *Balā*, lit. "calamity," (and not *jurm*) as the crime was not proved. Had it been proved, it might entail the penalty of death.

2 *Tamāshā karnā* gives an idea of enjoying a spectacle.

3 *Lage*; *vide* "Hindustani Stumbling-Blocks," XXII, 4.

straight from God into this world. You have just *now* even, shown us truth in your speech.

Wazīr : Get out of my sight—bitch! [Exit Zebā Khānum.] Shu'la! Tell me nothing but the truth.[1] Let me too know that you know all about the matter.

Shu'la Khānum : I swear by Your Honour's head that in this matter I am not in the least to blame. [While this is going on, Mas'ūd the eunuch enters, and standing behind the Wazīr pours out a cup of coffee and says—]

Mas'ūd : Coffee, sir.

Wazīr [turns round quickly and sees Mas'ūd with the coffee; he gives the cup an angry flip with his hand and the coffee is upset over the eunuch's clothes]: Get out, fool, ass! My mind is upset. Why in the devil should I take coffee? All right; I'm off (*chalā*) to the Khān. *He'll* clear up the difficulty. [Āqā Mas'ūd retires to a corner and begins to wipe the coffee off his clothes]. *Wazīr* [in the greatest perturbation]. Go, quick. Order my scarlet horse; tell them to saddle my chesnut cloak immediately. Make haste, make haste!

Āqā Mas'ūd : Certainly, certainly! By all means! I'll carry out Your Honour's commands to the letter. [Exit at a run.]

[After this the Wazīr too goes out.]

Shu'la Khānum : God is Great! I was in a strange predicament. Well, I've escaped. O God, I thank Thee! [While she is speaking Nisā Khānum enters. She addresses Nisā Khānum.] Nisā! A very strange thing has just happened. Do you, too, know anything of the matter? The Wazīr found Zebā Khānum and Tīmūr Āqā behind this *parda.*

Nisā Khānum : Is that a fact? What are you telling me? What on earth[2] was Zebā Khānum doing behind the *parda*?

Shu'la Khānum : I don't know when the whore came in and got behind the *parda*, but she saved my life. But there is

1 *Sach sach bayān karo.*

2 Note the position of *kyā.*

no doubt now that the Khān will kill Tīmūr Āqā. I cannot devise any plan at all to save him.

Nisā Khānum : Don't be afraid. What power has the Khān to kill Tīmūr Āqā? But I wish such a thing had not happened. Now the case won't stop here. Darling mother was asking after you, please go and see her. I will send Āqā Mas'ūd now to the Khān's darbār to find out all the news.

[Exit both.]

[The curtain falls.]

ACT III.

[Takes place in the *dīwān-khāna* or court-room of the Khān of Lankurān, on the sea-shore. The Khān is seated on a throne in the *tālār* [1] of the *dīwān-khāna.* Salīm Beg, the Master of the Ceremonies, is standing before him with a mace. On both sides, are the ministers and nobles of Lankurān drawn up in line. Ṣamad Beg, the chief of the farrāshes, and 'Azīz Āqā, the head-servant, are seated at the door with two or three body-servants. Below the *tālār* and near Qadīr Beg, the Deputy Master of the Ceremonies, are petitioners awaiting the summons to the Presence. The farrāshes are collected on one side of the *tālār.*]

Khān : It's a fine clear day. After *darbār* I should like to go for a short sail. It will be a diversion. 'Azīz Āqā, tell the boatmen to get the 'peacock-boat' ready.

'Azīz Āqā : On my head and eyes. [Exit.]

Khān : Salīm Beg! Order the complainants to be brought up.

Master of the Ceremonies [in a loud voice from inside the *tālār*]*:* Qadīr Beg! Bring up the complainants singly.

[Qadīr Beg brings up two men, complainant and defendant. They make their obeisance.]

Complainant : May I be the Khān's sacrifice! I have a petition to make.

[1] The *tālār* is a large open room or verandah opening on to a garden or court-yard. It has a plinth, sometimes several feet high.

K͟hān: Make the petition you have to make. Let me see what news you have brought, you fellow.

Complainant: May I be the K͟hān's sacrifice! To-day I took my horse to the river to water it. The horse broke loose and galloped off. This man was coming towards me. I called out, "Sir! For the sake of God stop the horse." He stooped, picked up a stone and threw it at the horse. The stone hit the horse in the eye and blinded [1] it. The horse is now no good; it is useless. I want compensation for the horse and he won't give it. He disputes with me.

K͟hān [turning to the plaintiff]: Fellow! Is this so?

Defendant: May I be your sacrifice; it is right, but your slave did not throw the stone on purpose.

K͟hān: What stuff are you talking? If you had had no intention how could you have picked up a stone and thrown it? Do you possess a horse of your own or not?

Defendant: I do, may I be your sacrifice!

K͟hān [addressing the complainant]: Fellow, go, and do you too throw a stone and blind the horse of the defendant,—"A tooth for a tooth, and an eye for an eye, and an ear for an ear, and for wounds retaliation." [2] This is no complicated case. Ṣamad Beg, order a farrāsh to go to the defendant's place and remain there until this person has exacted 'retaliation' for his horse.

[Ṣamad Beg makes an obeisance, and, leading both away, hands them over to a farrāsh and returns.]

K͟hān: Salīm Beg! Tell me, is there any other petitioner? If there is, produce him. Be quick. To-day we would take the air in a boat.

Salīm Beg: Qadīr Beg! If there is any other complainant, bring him up.

[Qadīr Beg brings up two other individuals.]

K͟hān: Oh Dominion! Is there anything in the world more troublesome than thou? Other people have merely to think

[1] *Kānā*, blind in one eye, one-eyed.

[2] A misquotation from the *Qur,ān*.

each one for himself, whereas *We* have to care for thousands of God's creatures and give them justice. From the first day of Our rule up to the present moment, *We* have never yet turned away any petitioner from *Our* door.

Salīm Beg: The blessings and prayers of all these creatures of God are the reward of all Your Honour's exertions. In truth, all this people is regarded by Your Honour in the light of Your own offspring. The prosperity of Lankurān is all due to the blessing of Your justice.

[The petitioners come forward and bow.]

Complainant: May I be the K͟hān's sacrifice! My brother was sick. This *individual* is a doctor.[1] I fee'd him two rupees. I brought him to my brother's bed in hopes he would cure him. As soon as he came he bled him, and no sooner did the blood come out than my brother died. Now when I ask the brute to, at least, give me back my money, he does not even *talk* about giving it back. What does he say but, "Had I not bled him, it would have been worse still." Set aside giving me back my money, he demands *more* from me. I ask Your Honour's help and justice. May I be Your sacrifice!

K͟hān [addressing the defendant]: Ḥakīm Ṣāḥib! Supposing you had not bled him, what worse could have happened than did happen?

Defendant; May I be the K͟hān's sacrifice! This person's brother was afflicted with the deadly malady of dropsy. Had I not bled him he would without doubt have died in six months' time. By relieving him of blood, I have saved the complainant [2] from the useless expense and worry of six months.

K͟hān: Ḥakīm Ṣāḥib! From what you say it appears that you have a further claim against this man?

Doctor: Yes, sir,[3] may I be Your Honour's sacrifice! If Your Honour gives me justice—undoubtedly.

K͟hān [addressing the courtiers]: Oh Allah! I do not in

1 Note that this villagers's speech is full of provincialisms.

2 *Isko.*

3 *Jī hāṅ ḥuẓūr.*

the least know how to settle the case to the satisfaction of both parties. Never in my whole life have[1] I ever seen, or even heard of, a case as complicated as this.

A Courtier : May I be Your sacrifice! Respect towards physicians is incumbent on us; they confer benefits on the community. Let an order be given to this man to bestow a robe of honour on the doctor and so satisfy his claims. Your devoted servant knows this doctor well. He is a skilled physiclau.

Kh̲ān *:* If the doctor is an acquaintance of yours then let it be as you suggest. [Addressing the complainant] Go. Give the doctor a cloak and satisfy his claims. Ṣamad Beg! send a farrāsh with them to obtain a cloak from this person and hand it over to the doctor.

[Ṣamad Beg withdraws. Just then the Wazīr enters puffing and blowing. He takes his pencase out of his pocket and lays it on the ground before the Kh̲ān.]

Wazīr *:* May I be Your sacrifice! I have done with the Wazīrship; it is enough for me. I have been rewarded for my services. Now please entrust the office to whomsoever you consider fitted for it. I must now bid farewell to this country and wander wretchedly from door to door.

Kh̲ān [astonished]: Wazīr Ṣāḥib! Well, tell me, what is the matter? What has happened? Why thus?

Wazīr *:* May I be Your sacrifice! To-day all over the face of the earth the justice and humanity of Your Highness is publicly proclaimed. From awe of You no one of Your subjects dare disturb a single hair even, of any poor man in the dominion. But kindly look to this, how fearless of You is Tīmūr Āqā, the son of Your brother. In broad daylight he enters the house of a person like me and makes an attempt against the honour of his wife.

Kh̲ān [in a passion]: Wazīr Ṣāḥib! What are you saying?

[1] He uses the Pluperfect to indicate a time anterior to the Preterite, *i.e.*, he has just seen (Preterite in Urdu) the present complicated case.

Tīmūr Āqā has been as bold as this ? What is the meaning of it ?

Wazīr : If I represent aught but the truth, may Your salt break out on my body in leprous sores. I have myself seen it with these eyes of mine. I seized [1] him to bring him into Your Presence, but he jerked himself free and escaped.

Khān : Ṣamad Beg! Go quickly—summon Tīmūr Āqā here —but tell him nothing. [Ṣamad Beg bows and goes out.] Wazīr Ṣāḥib! Have no anxiety, I will give you such redress that all will take warning from it.

Wazīr : May I be Your sacrifice ! Former kings spared not even their children or kin in the cause of justice. Renowned Caliphs administered condign punishment to their children even for a single unlawful look at a woman.[2] Sulṭān Maḥmūd of Ghaznī with his own hand struck off the head of one of his courtiers [3] for a similar offence; and hence, in spite of the lapse of time the renown of his great [4] justice remains fresh in the world.

Khān [addressing the Wazīr] : Wazīr Ṣāḥib ! You will now [5] this moment see that Your Khān is not the least behind the great Caliphs and Sulṭān Maḥmūd of Ghaznī in justice, especially in the present instance.

[Ṣamad Beg and Tīmūr Āqā now [6] enter the darbār, and bow.]

Khān [addressing Tīmūr Āqā]: Did I not order you not to appear before me wearing a dagger ?

Tīmūr Āqā : But I have not got a dagger on.

Khān : I thought you had one on. Well : what were you doing in the Wazīr's house ? [Tīmūr Āqā hangs his head.]

1 Lit., I had seized him [but he got away]. Pluperfect to indicate a time anterior to a Preterite.

2 *Nā-maḥram*, adj., is any man or woman, stranger or relation, with whom marriage might be possible. *Maḥram* is applied to very near relations whom it is forbidden to marry.

3 *Muqarrab* is a courtier or any person who has a seat near to the throne.

4 Two synonyms. 5 *Abhī abhī ;* emphatic. 6 *Itne meṅ.*

Do you want me to be disgraced everywhere through having a vagabond nephew like you? Now I no longer require a nephew like you. Farrāshes! The rope! [Several farrāshes present themselves with a Kashmir shawl.] Cast the shawl round the neck of this shameless ill-doer, throw him on the ground.

[The farrāshes get ready to cast the shawl round his neck. The eyes of all present in the darbār fill with tears.]

Master of the Ceremonies and all the Khān's servants : May I be the Khān's sacrifice! He is young. Please pardon him this time.

Khān : I swear by the blessed soul of my sainted father, never never will I forgive him. [Addressing the farrāshes] Cast the shawl.

[The farrāshes come a little nearer. All lose their self-control and begin to weep unrestrainedly, and then, abasing themselves in the dust, they entreat the Khān humbly—] Mercy, Oh Khān! Spare the life of Tīmūr Āqā! Let there be an order for him to be released as a sacrifice for You. He is the only son of his mother. [They weep and wail.]

Khān : I ask pardon of God![1] It cannot be, it can never be. [Beside himself with rage, to the farrāshes] Sons of pigs! Haven't I ordered you to throw him down?

[The farrāshes, shawl in hand, move a little nearer. Tīmūr Āqā quickly puts his hand behind him, produces a pistol and aims it at the farrāshes who shy off him in perturbation. Under cover of this confusion, Tīmūr Āqā springs aside and makes off.]

Khān [seeing him going]: Take him! Seize him! Don't let him go! [All precipitately pretend[2] to rush at him but no one goes in pursuit.] [Scowling, to the nobles] Not one of you is worthy of Our favour. Why did you let the bastard escape? [No one answers.] Ṣamad Beg! [Ṣamad Beg comes forward.]

1 This exclamation is used in denials, refusals, and when expressing disbelief.

2 *Chāhte hain* here means "make a show of," *i.e.*, they go through all the gestures of attack but refrain from the reality.

Quickly take fifty mounted men and go in search of Tīmūr Āqā. Trace him out in whatever corner of the earth he may be, arrest him, and bring him into my presence, handcuffed. Till I slay him, there will be no peace for this province and no rest for my heart.

Ṣamad Beg : I obey. [Goes out.]

Khān [addressing the nobles]: Go. You are dismissed. [All go off.] 'Azīz Āqā! ['Azīz Āqā comes forward.] Is the peacock-boat ready?

'Azīz Āqā : Yes, my Lord; it is ready.

Khān [rising]: Wazīr! Depart now. Set your mind at rest. Have no anxiety. Your wrong shall be redressed. Take this ring and give it to Nisā Khānum. I sent men to-day to the jeweller's especially, and they chose and brought this. Busy yourself with the preparations for the marriage. Within a week it must be celebrated.

Wazīr : By all means I will carry out Your orders.

[Makes his obeisance and goes out. The Khān and 'Azīz Āqā get into the peacock-boat and go for a sail.]

[The curtain falls.]

ACT IV.

[Takes place in Shu'la Khānum's room. Shu'la Khānum and Nisā Khānum are seated talking to each other in a state of great perturbation and expectation.]

Nisā Khānum : I don't know what has happened to him![1] Mas'ūd has not yet returned, nor has any news reached us. My heart beats.

Shu'la Khānum . Why are you so nervous? What power has the Khān to injure a hair even of Tīmūr Āqā's head?

Nisā Khānum : It's true he can't do him any harm: what I fear is separation between Tīmūr Āqā and myself. I would rather die than endure that.

[Āqā Mas'ūd now enters.]

[1] *Un kā* means Tīmūr Āqā. Nisā Khānum, being his betrothed, would not take his name.

Shu'la Khānum : Āqā Mas'ūd ! Just say—what has happened ?

Āqā Mas'ūd : What should have happened ? The Wazīr petitioned the Khān. The Khān summoned Tīmūr Āqā. He wanted to strangle him. Tīmūr Āqā pointed a pistol at the farrāshes and scattered them, and escaped. The Khān has ordered fifty rank and file to find Tīmūr Āqā and bring him handcuffed to be beheaded. Now bodies of men are running about all about the city and searching every house.

[Nisā Khānum in great distress heaves a deep sigh. At this moment the door opens and in walks Tīmūr Āqā.]

Shu'la Khānum : Oh, how awful ! What is this ? You here—and why ? How did you come ? You have the heart of a lion [1]—moreover you care nothing for your life.

Tīmūr Āqā [smilingly] : What has happened that I should fear for my life ?

Shu'la Khānum : You doubt about something happening ? What has *not* happened ? The Khān has despatched men in all directions to track you out and arrest you and carry you off to be killed. Why then do you come here in this imperturbed way ? Āqā Mas'ūd, for God's sake just go out and keep watch that no one may come here.

[Āqā Mas'ūd goes out.]

Tīmūr Āqā : What ! Did you think that fear of being killed would prevent me from coming to-day to see Nisā Khānum ? For her sake I have played with my life. I have not come now without reason. It is my intention to carry off (*bhagākar*) Nisā Khānum to-night, to some other place. I cannot now leave her here for an instant: your husband has behaved treacherously towards me. I cannot now by any means leave my betrothed in his house.

Shu'la Khānum : You are right—I too agree. But it was not well for you to come here in broad daylight. Why, don't

[1] In Persia *shīr* (in India pronounced *sher*) is a "lion"; but in India *sher* means "tiger."

you yourself know that Zebā K͟hānum has set people to watch me everywhere? Give her the least opportunity and [1] she takes *your* life and disgraces *me* utterly.[2] The best thing for you to do now, is to go away. At midnight, when everybody is sound asleep, be here at the door with the horses and men. I will punctually bring Nisā K͟hānum and hand her over to your charge with a "Take her and bear her away on your horse."

Tīmūr Āqā: Nisā K͟hānum! Do you too agree?

Nisā K͟hānum: Certainly, I agree most heartily. What other course is there but this?

[At this moment Mas'ūd Āqā calls through the door.] God's protection! The Wazīr Ṣāḥib has arrived!

Shu'la K͟hānum and Nisā K͟hānum [losing their heads]: Oh, how awful! God protect us! Āqā! hide behind the *parda*. See! [3] I will concoct some plan to get this tyrant out of the room.

Tīmūr Āqā [looking quite undisturbed and speaking calmly]: Never again [4] will I go and hide behind the curtain. If he is coming, let him come. If he sees me here, he *will* see me here.

Shu'la K͟hānum [falling at his feet and in the utmost disorder]: For the sake of God don't run into danger! By the soul of your sainted father go behind this *parda!*

Tīmūr Āqā: Never.

Āqā Mas'ūd [putting his head in at the door, again calls out]: Alas, alas! the Wazīr is here.

Shu'la K͟hānum: May I be Your sacrifice—Pity *us*. If the Wazīr sees you here now, he will never let us remain alive.

Tīmūr Āqā: Very well. I go for *your* sakes.

[He goes behind the *parda*. A moment later the Wazīr enters.)

Wazīr: It's well you are both here; I have something important to say to both of you; listen attentively. Shu'la K͟hānum! You know how much my position and yours will

1 Note the use of *ki* for *aur*.
2 Two synonyms.
3 *Dekhiye* is here an interjection.
4 *Ab to*.

be bettered when I have married your sister to the Khān. Ought you not then to be careful not to allow your good name to be doubted? Why do you give people an opportunity to say that the sister-in-law of the Khān has communications with strange men?

Shu'la Khānum [slowly and with great calmness]: Kindly inform me with what *nā-mahram* men I have communications.

Wazīr: Let us suppose Tīmūr Āqā, whom I saw in your room.

Shu'lā Khānum: Yes, yes; he was hiding behind this curtain with your wife Zebā Khānum.

Wazīr: It is true. I don't in the least suspect *you.* The fault must have been with Zebā Khānum. I merely mention the matter to you that you may keep right in your conduct so that no one may have an opportunity of saying anything against your name before the Khān, lest his heart should turn from Nisā Khānum. He is now very much enamoured of Nisā Khānum. He has ordered me to busy myself about the marriage, which is to take place next week. He has sent this ring as a present; Nisā Khānum, come, take it, put it on your finger.

[Places the ring in Nisā Khānum's palm.]

Nisā Khānum: A girl whose sister is not respected, cannot be fit for the Khān. Take back this ring, and when you find a girl a fit match for the Khān put it on *her* finger.

[She throws the ring on the ground in front of the Wazīr and goes out.]

Wazīr [calling after her]: Here listen, come, girl; how was I suspicious of your sister? I merely gave her a small piece of advice.[1]

Shu'lā Khānum: But could you not have given this advice to your wife Zebā Khānum?

Wazīr: Yes; of course. To-morrow I will speak to her with greater harshness than this.

[1] *Naṣīḥat* "admonition."

Shu'lā Khānum : Why to-morrow? Cannot you go to her to-day?

Wazīr : To-day there is no great necessity, for even admitting that Tīmūr Āqā was her 'friend,' *he* has got his deserts. One of two things will happen; either he will be arrested and killed in the presence of the Khān, or else he will flee the country and wander from door to door miserably. Now it is not necessary for you ever to mention his name before me. We must now busy ourselves with the preparations for Nisā Khānum's marriage.

Shu'lā Khānum : Then please go to darling mother's room and speak to *her*. This has nothing to do with *me*.

Wazīr : Why don't you call your darling mother here? We can talk to her here. [At this moment the door opens and Parī Khānum and Nisā Khānum enter. The Wazīr addresses Parī Khānum.] It is well you have happened to come here. Come, please sit down.

Parī Khānum : May I take your calamities on me! This is not a time for sitting down. If you go off now, I shan't get a glimpse of you again. Listen to me; I want to tell you something. By the grace of God you are such a busy man that I never get a glimpse of you.[1]

Wazīr : Of course. Especially lately I have had no time to scratch my head even. But please tell me what it is you really want.

Parī Khānum : May I be your sacrifice! It was no great matter. I went to the diviner Qurbān to get an amulet; if God wills by its blessing a son may be born to Shu'la Khānum in your house. The soothsayer wrote an amulet for me and said, "Cook *khīr*[2] to the amount of three times the Wazīr's head and distribute it to the poor and needy." I must *at once* cook that amount of *khīr*, for the auspicious moment is passing.

Wazīr : Well, you have taken upon yourself a strange task. Dear mother, as long as my head is on my body, how can you know the amount of it?

1 Lit. "that I long for a sight of you (and can't get it)." 2 *Khīr*.

Parī Khānum: May I be your sacrifice! It is no difficult matter. The diviner explained the method to me. He said I must take a deep pot and cover your head well with it, and the pot which contains your head easily, will be considered the measure of your head. Nisā Khānum! go and fetch a pot.

[Nisā Khānum goes and brings a small pot which Āqā Mas'ūd had placed there ready.[1] Parī Khānum gently puts out her hand, and quickly takes off the Wazīr's hat.]

Wazīr: Although this fuss is foolish,[2] still I cannot make any objection. One must follow out the instructions of soothsayers. God grant Shu'la Khānum's desire may be fulfilled!

Parī Khānum: Oh God, amen! Nisā Khānum, place the pot over his head.

[Nisā Khānum reverses the pot over the Wazīr's head, but it will not come below his eyebrows. Nisā Khānum gives it a thump on the top, to make it go down.]

Wazīr [lifting up both his hands]: Oh! horrible! What are you doing? You're hurting my nose.

[He removes the pot from his head.]

Parī Khānum [quickly]: Daughter, bring another pot.

[Nisā Khānum runs off and fetches another pot in haste.]

Wazīr: Dear mother! Kindly postpone this vexatious business (*bakheṛā*) to some other time; I have now something very important to tell you.

Parī Khānum: No, my son! This can't be. The auspicious moment will be lost. Let me take your calamities upon myself; don't be vexed. It is the work of but a moment. I am taking all this trouble (*koshisheṅ*) merely on *your* account. [*Crying*]. Shall I leave this world without having seen in my old age a child in Shu'lā Khānum's arms (*god*)? [Her eyes wet with tears, she turns to Nisā Khānum.] Child, reverse the pot over his head. You ought to have brought this pot at first.

[1] Note the force of *rakhnā*: *vide* "Hindustani Manual," p. 86 (*d*).

[2] *Fuẓūl* a milder term than *ḥimāqat* or *bewuqūfī*, words that would not be polite to a mother-in-law.

[Nisā Khānum puts the pot on his head and it comes down to his neck. Parī Khānum rapidly makes a sign to Shu'la Khānum towards the *parda*. Shu'la Khānum gently lifts the *parda*, and leading out Tīmūr Āqā puts him through the door. Nisā Khānum then lifts up the pot from the Wazīr's head.]

Wazīr : Ah, well. Dear mother, now sit down while [1] I talk to you.

Parī Khānum : Yes, my son.

[She is just going to sit down when a noise is heard from the court-yard and immediately afterwards Tīmūr Āqā enters with a pistol in his hand. The Wazīr, at the sight of Tīmūr Āqā, is seized with a violent trembling.]

Tīmūr Āqā : Ungrateful traitor! You now are set on having my life taken for no reason. I am not now likely to die without first killing you.

[He points the pistol at the Wazīr.]

Shu'lā Khānum [falling at Tīmūr Āqā's feet and imploring him]: Tīmūr Āqā! Pity! Oh, lower your hand; restrain your anger.

[Tīmūr Āqā lowers his hand. At this moment Ṣamad Beg and a number of soldiers enter and halt by the door.]

Tīmūr Āqā : Ṣamad Beg! What is your purpose? What do you intend doing?

Ṣamad Beg : I am the servant both of your revered father and of you. How is it possible for me to act disrespectfully towards you? But your Honour well knows what the order of the Khān is. It is my duty to take you before him.

Tīmūr Āqā : You will not take me alive before him, but you may take him my head. Only my head won't fall into any-one's possession very easily. Please begin [2]—come and take it if you can.

Ṣamad Beg : Respected Sir, I admit [3] that you can shoot me,

[1] *Tā ki* "in order that, so that."

[2] Musilms say *Bismi'llah* when commencing any work; hence *bism-illah karnā* = "to commence."

[3] Preterite.

but behind me are fifty soldiers. You can't possibly kill all of them.[1] But such discussion is idle. The Khān's anger is appeased. He has promised that he will not injure you in any way.

Tīmūr Āqā : I trust neither his word nor his deed. When has he ever stood by his word that one should believe any promise of his ? I stick to what I said.

[At this moment an uproar is heard from the court-yard outside. Salīm Beg, the Master of Ceremonies, and Riẓā 'Alī Beg, Tīmūr Āqā's foster-brother, enter the room.]

Salīm Beg : Ṣamad Beg, back! Tīmūr Āqā, may you live long! Your uncle, the Khān, went for a sail. Suddenly a contrary wind arose and the boat upset and sank, taking him with it. Now the people are assembled round the justice-hall, awaiting your approach. Please go there and take possession of the throne of your late (*marḥūm*) father.

Tīmūr Āqā : Well, Riẓā, is this so ? [2]

Riẓā : Yes, sir, it is, may I be your sacrifice! If it be your will, let us all go there.

[The Wazīr and Ṣamad Beg come forward and prostrate [3] themselves in entreaty.]

Wazīr and *Ṣamad Beg :* May we be Your Honour's sacrifice! Spare our lives.

Tīmūr Āqā : Ṣamad Beg, rise and stand aside. [Ṣamad Beg rises and goes to one side.] Wazīr, Our [4] reason for coming to your house was that I had, and still have, a great attachment to your sister-in-law Nisā Khānum, and it was Our intention, in accordance with the command of God and the Prophet, the sacred law, and the girl's own desire,

[1] Emphatic denial expressed by a query; *vide* "Hindustani Manual," p. 25 (*f*).

[2] Tīmūr would believe his own foster-brother.

[3] *Sijda* is properly prostration in prayer; *vide* "Hugh's Dictionary of Islam."

[4] Tīmūr at once assumes the Royal plural, and throughout this speech is very pompous.

to enter into the bond of matrimony with her ; but you, for some imaginary hope, desired to unite her with the late unhallowed,[1] and on this account we could not inform you of Our heart's desire. This was the reason you entertained evil suspicions of me and fell into the design of killing me. "But Heaven's decree makes vain the plans of men.[2]" The Divine Justice which justly rewards every man, rich or poor, according to his works, has set free the right-doers and frustrated your intentions. Now We, seeing the mal-administration and the evil practices committed by you with regard to the peasants in the time of your power, must not again entrust you with the office of Wazīr or allow you to remain in your former employment ; for when evil habits and propensities have taken deep root in a person's nature, they can in no wise be eradicated, and no hope can be entertained that he will ever strive for the welfare of the people. But since you have been nourished by the salt of Our House, We close Our eyes entirely to your past offences. Henceforth, for the remainder of your life, you shall remain Our pensioner, spending your days in ease and tranquillity in the bosom of your family. But inasmuch as the good and welfare of the people and the State are ever before Our eyes, never expect that the office of Wazīr will again be held by you ; for to give the administration of the country into hands of people like you, is remote from humanity and justice. Whoever wishes to bring the affairs of the State into good order, and to improve the condition of the peasants and the gentry, must of necessity set aside and remove uninformed and incompetent and self-interested people, and commit the well-being of the State and the Nation to experienced, and competent, and upright men : let him not give over the administration of the affairs of God's creatures into the keeping of a person in whose nature greed and corrup-

[1] *G͟hair-marḥūm*, a phrase invented by Tīmūr. *Marḥūm*, "pitied or blessed," is used for any dead Muslim by Muslims, and sometimes for Christians also.

[2] 'Man proposes but God disposes.'

tion are engrained, one who gives judgments contrary to peoples' rights and merely with a view to his own interests and profits. Should one act so, then the administration of the peasants and the country will proceed with regularity, and the inhabitants, whether officials or private persons, will spend their days in peace and quietness. Well, at all events for the present, there is no time for prolonging Our discourse. We must now set about the necessary preparations for Nisā K͟hānum's marriage. We hope (*in shā Allah* [1]) that, in the coming week, the instructions for the marriage ceremony will be given, and matters brought to a speedy conclusion. Well, dear mother, and sister Shu'la K͟hānum, adieu! Occupy yourselves in your respective affairs.[2]

Parī K͟hānum and Shu'la K͟hānum : May God prolong Your Highness's reign! God grant your rule may last a hundred years!

[Tīmūr Āqā, accompanied by all the nobles, leaves the room: and the Wazīr remains behind in a state of dismay.]

Soldiers [with a loud shout in the court-yard without]: Prosperity attend on Tīmūr K͟hān.

[*Curtain.*]

[1] Lit. "if God pleases."

[2] The whole of this speech is purposely verbose to indicate Tīmūr Āqā's increased importance.

PART III.

HISTORICAL EVENTS.

1. AMĪR NĀṢIR-UD-DĪN SABUKTIGĪN.

In the country to the North-West of the Panjab, a ruler named Alptigīn made his capital in a city called Ghaznī. Once a merchant brought to his darbār a Turk slave. The Amīr approved of him and purchased him, and gave him the name of Sabuktigīn. The boy was intelligent and smart and exercised his thinking faculties in his work. Gradually he became Commander-in-Chief, and, advancing step by step, at last married the Amīr's daughter.

When Sabuktigīn was a slave, he was very fond of *shikār*. He once saw a doe with a fawn, grazing about in the jungle, and chased them on his horse. The doe escaped, but the fawn fell into his hands. He secured it, tied it on the pommel of his saddle, and started for the city. When he had proceeded a short distance, he looked round and saw that the mother, through her affection, was closely following him looking up at him, very disturbed on account of her young one. Sabuktigīn took pity on her and released the young. The doe started for the forest with her young, and Sabuktigīn remained standing and watching her. He noticed that she went a few paces and stopped, and then looked round towards him as though she were thanking him. That night he heard a voice in his dreams saying to him, "O Sabuktigīn! thou hadst pity on that poor dumb animal: God was pleased: the order for sovereignty has been written against thy name. Remember (*dekh*) to treat God's creatures (*i.e.* thy subjects) with the same kindness."

When Alptigīn died, his son succeeded him, but he was a boy and the duty of ruling remained with Subuktigīn only (*hī*). A year later, the boy too died. Subuktigīn by his goodness had won peoples' hearts.[1] At last, by the consent of all, he became Ruler, and began to administer the country and strengthen his forces.

At this period, a Brahman, by name Jaipāl, was ruling in Lahore. When he saw the advance of the Muslim power (*Islām*) towards India, he deemed it necessary to stem it. He collected a great army of horse and foot and elephants, and. marching to the attack, reached the borders of Sabuktigīn's territory. On the other hand Sabuktigīn advanced with an army to meet him. A battle was fought. By chance at that time heavy rain began to fall, and the cold was so intense that the blood froze in peoples' veins (*badan meṅ jam-gayā*), and they remained inactive as they were.

The people of India had never experienced (seen) such a state of things, and were much distressed (*ghabrā,e*), and despaired of life.

Jaipāl sent a message of peace. Sabuktigīn had pity on their condition and wished to accept the offer of peace, but his son Maḥmūd was with him, and he remonstrated,[2] saying that the intense cold was heavenly aid, and that they had won a victory without the necessity of drawing their swords; that if their adversaries (*ḥarīf*) made peace and got off, all the wealth and resources that were with them would be lost without reason (*muft*). The father agreed to what his son had said, and declined the overtures of peace. The Raja sent word (*kahlā-bhejā*) to the following effect: "You know not the custom of the braves of India. When they despair of life, they consume by fire whatever possessions they have; blind their elephants, horses, and cattle; cast their women and children into the fire; and then fight till they bite the dust. Such a time has now arrived. If you make peace, it is your clemency; if not, you will regret it, and will find, instead of wealth and spoil, only a heap of ashes." On

1 *Dil meṅ ghar kar-rakhā. Rakhnā* gives the idea of beforehand; *vide* "Hind. Man.," p. 86 (*d*).

2 *Samjhāyā.*

hearing this Maḥmūd too consented (*rāẓī hū.ā*). Peace was made on the condition that the Raja should surrender fifty elephants, a large sum of money, and part of his dominions. The arrangements for all these things could not be made on the spot (*wahīṅ*). The Raja said: "Whatever is present [1] with me, is at your service (*ḥāẓir hai* [2]). To collect the remainder, let the Amīr send trusty agents with me; on reaching Lahore every arrangement will be carried out." Sabuktigīn agreed.

On reaching Lahore, Jaipāl repudiated what he had promised and imprisoned Sabuktigīn's men. When Sabuktigīn heard this, he refused to credit it (*—ko yaqīn na-āyā*). At last, when he became certain of the truth, he became enraged, and marched with an army against India. Jaipāl too made preparations. He wrote to the whole of the Rajas of India, that 'they knew [3] that the Panjab was the gate of their own terrritories; and that if it broke, it would fare ill with them.' All sent armies. They despatched treasure and munitions of war in profusion. Thus a great host of Hindus was collected. Jaipāl started at the head of these, to oppose Sabuktigīn. When both armies came opposite each other, the fight waxed hot. The braves of both sides gave up their lives for the sake of their honour (*nām*). The Hindu army had fought hard without cessation since the early morning; but as day declined confusion (*ghabrāhaṭ*) appeared in their ranks. At this juncture Sabuktigīn made an attack with his whole force. Jaipāl was defeated, and the army was so uprooted that it could not again make a stand. A large quantity of loot fell into the Muslims' hands. After ruling for twenty years, Subuktigīn departed from this world having founded a dynasty in his family.

1 *Maujūd, vide* "Hind. Man.," p. 36 (*a*).
2 *Ḥāẓir, vide* "Hind. Man.," p. 36 (*a*).
3 Direct narration.

2. SULṬĀN MAḤMŪD-I GHAZNAVĪ.

Sabuktigīn was succeeded by his son Maḥmūd. At that time there was a certain very brave and old Sardār, with whom Maḥmūd was annoyed on account of several acts of his. He marched against him with an army. The old Sardār opposed him, but was at last besieged in a fort (*qil'a-band honā*). Maḥmūd placed his army round it and closed the approaches on all sides. One day he gave orders for an assault. He had the elephants' heads (*mastak*) protected by shields, and ordered them to be driven at the gates. The first elephant had no sooner run against the gates, than the alarmed Sardār came out. He came before Maḥmūd, and, dismounting, placed (rubbed) his white beard on the hoof of Maḥmūd's horse saying, "O Sulṭān! Forgive. In what I have done, I have done ill." Maḥmūd liked the address (word) "Sulṭān" and began to write "Sulṭān Maḥmūd" in his farmāns.

The lesson of India that Maḥmūd had learnt from his father, he never forgot; he invaded India several times. For this, he had two reasons; the first, to spread Islām; the second, to collect the wealth and stores of India. The table of the wealth of India was ever spread in his sight. Whenever (*jab*) he got an opportunity, it was that place (*idhar hī*) he invaded. He carried off as loot, cash, jewels, ornaments of gold and silver, and many costly stuffs.

He invaded India sixteen or seventeen times, but twelve of his invasions are famous. The greatest invasion was that against Somnāth. That city was situated (*ābād thā*) on the sea, and was very prosperous, and was filled full of wealth (*mālā-māl*). Under its loftly fortress the waves billowed, and dashed against its lofty ramparts.

X Inside the fortress was a noble and spacious (*wasī'*) temple, hundreds of years old. Fifty-six columns supported its roof, and these were decorated with paintings, and creepers and flowers of studded jewels. Such (this) was the temple of Somnāth Jī.[1] In it only one lamp burnt, night and day. Its light fell on the jewels; by their lustre the whole building

[1] Hindus add *Jī* to the names of all their sacred places, while Muslim add *sharīf*.

scintillated. On a golden chain were suspended bells, and at the time of worship (*pūjā*), these were shaken [tr. verb, 3rd pers. pl.] to warn all, that it was the time of worship. There were two thousand Brahmins, officiating priests; five hundred women, and three hundred barbers[1] for 'barbering' the pilgrims. At an eclipse, more than two lākhs of pilgrims used to collect there. Rajas had presented to the temples, as church-property, nearly two thousand villages.[2] Rajas and Maharajas used to send their daughters to serve in the temple,[3] and used also to send offerings of ornaments,[4] jewels, and costly stuffs. In short, the wealth of the temple was beyond computation.

Maḥmūd equipped an army, choosing heroic sawārs and intrepidly brave soldiers, and started. With him were thousands of Muslims that had drawn the sword merely for the Faith and thought it holy martyrdom to give up their lives in the cause of Islām. A desert lay in the way of the army, in which, for many marches, there was not a blade of grass nor a drop of water. People were at the point of death,[5] but still that determined man did not waver.

He passed through it, and crossing forests and mountains, reached his destination. Here several Rajas with large armies met him and the fight was hot. On one side fought the Faith; on the other the *Dharam* offered a stubborn resistance. So many Hindus and Muslims were killed by the sword (*kaṭe*) that to count them was no easy task.

At last the Brahmins fought so desperately that the Muslims lost heart. Maḥmūd even lost his head. He could do nothing else but quit the army, place his head on the ground, and

1 Why *nā,ī* ?

2 Translate literally, and write out this sentence, and mark its construction; or better still learn it by heart.

3 And be prostituted by the Brahmins.

4 *Zewar*, ornaments, specially of gold and silver.

5 Note the idiom.

pray[1] to God. After a short time,[2] he got up from his knees, and exhorted his army, and, raising its courage, gave an order to charge. The Muslims suddenly raised their swords and galloping their horses burst upon (*ṭūṭ-paṛnā*) their enemies. A hot and tumultuous fight took place.[3] At length Maḥmūd's good fortune (*iqbāl*) had its usual effect: the Hindus fled, and the Muslims were victorious. Seeing the battle-field empty, the garrison in the fort too lost all heart. They had kept ready (*lagā-rakhnā*) boats in the sea, on the far side of the fort. They embarked in them, raised anchor, and fled. The city, the fort, the temple, and all the wealth of the place, fell into Maḥmūd's hands.

Although[4] Maḥmūd had vanquished very far-off cities in India, still (*magar*) he had no intention of remaining in India (*yahāṅ*), but settled a governor in Lahore. By the loot of India, he had made Ghaznī, situated in a barren mountain tract, so prosperous and flourishing (*ābād*), that it was like an enchanted city. Men from every country, skilled craftsmen of every art (*fann*)[5] were there. He built a fort and named it the 'Turquoise Palace'[6]; compared with its enamel-work (?) jewels appeared to lack lustre (*—kī rangat phīkī ma'lūm hotī thī*). The palace and darbār-chambers in it reminded one of fairy-land.

He built such a congregational mosque[7] that, on account of the splendour of its decoration, it became known as the 'Bride of Heaven.' Alongside of it, he built a college of similar dimensions and dignity. He furnished (*sajānā*) its libraries with rare and costly books,[8] and learned and cultured[9] men were appointed to spread abroad the light

[1] What is the difference between *du'ā* and *namāz*?

[2] The meaning is that he remained on his knees some time.

[3] Note idiom with *paṛnā*.

[4] Note the position of *agarchi*.

[5] *Fann* "art," and *hunar* "craft."

[6] *Qaṣr*.

[7] *Jāmi' Masjid* (or *jum'a Masjid*).

[8] *i.e.* MSS.

[9] *Fāẓil* is more than *'ālim*; the former is an M.A. to the latter's B.A.

of knowledge. All followed the Sulṭān's fancy (*shauq*) for building and furnishing, and, in a short time, many noble mansions came into existence. Hundreds of mosques, colleges, serais, and monasteries[1] arose. In every house (*ghar ghar*) there was wealth and great store of riches. During his time (*'ahd*) G͟haznī recalled to mind India, for in the houses of even poor men three or four Hindustani-speaking slave-girls and slave-men were to be found. In the G͟haznī bazars (these) creatures of God were sold for two rupees each. /

Maḥmūd was so fond of wealth that some mention of this defect is made in every history-book. Towards the end of his life he got news of a certain person reputed to be wealthy. He had him arrested and brought before him. When the poor fellow came before him, Maḥmūd said: "We have heard that you are irreligious and unorthodox." He replied (*'arẓ kī*), "Thy devoted slave is free from this crime, but he[2] has this defect that his wealth is great. Deprive me[2] of it, but not of my good name." Maḥmūd placed his wealth in the Royal treasury and wrote a certificate to the effect that he was a very good and orthodox person.

In spite of these defects, he now and then exhibited a royal magnanimity.[3] For instance, some Baluchis had seized a fort, and by occupying it, harassed the roads. Once a caravan was robbed and a fine young man killed. His old mother came weeping and beating her breast into Māḥmūd's darbār and lodged a complaint. Maḥmūd said, "What can I do? How is it possible to govern properly places so far distant?" She replied, "Oh Sulṭān! If thou canst not manage to rule so great a country, why didst thou take it and keep it?" Maḥmūd was left without an answer (*kuchh jawāb na ban-āyā*). He immediately gave orders for an army to go and capture the fort from the robbers, and that until the fort was taken (Aor. with negative[4]), a cavalry regiment should continue to escort every caravan.

1 What is a *K͟hānqāh* ? 2 This change of person is incorrect.
3 *Ḥauṣala*, lit. crop. 4 *Vide* "Hind. Man.," p. 212 (*b*) and p. 132 (*b*).

He once invaded some territory. A young boy was the rightful heir and his mother ruled for him. When news of Maḥmūd's having assembled an army became noised abroad, that woman of sense sent him word as follows:—"If the Sulṭān defeats me, then in all the proclamations of victory (*fataḥ-nāma*)[1] that he will send out to cities be will write, 'I have wrested the territory from a widow woman.' Should he be defeated, it will be a great disgrace to him. But, however, should he preserve her country as it is, all will say he has given her a crown."[2] *Maḥmūd* understood her, and gave up all thoughts of the expedition.

He collected many learned and erudite men in Ghaznī. He was very fond of poetry too; but by what he did to Fridausi, he has cast a stain on his reputation for appreciation. It is said that, when he ordered him to compose the *Shāh-Nāma*, he promised him in reward a gold piece (*ashrafī*) for each couplet. The poor poet grew old in composing his work. When, in thirty years, he had composed sixty thousand couplets, and presented the book, Maḥmūd wanted to give him rupees instead of *ashrafīs*. Fridausi received a great shock at seeing all his labour wasted. By writing a satire on Maḥmūd he relieved his feelings (*dil kā bukhār nikālnā*) and fled from the spot. After some days, some one quoted (*paṛhnā*) a verse of his aptly in *darbār*. Maḥmūd's heart smote him; and he regretted what he had done. On the spot, he directed that cash should be sent to Fridausi according to the correct account. But alas, when Maḥmūd's men with the money reached the gate of Fridausi's city, they met a bier; they learnt that Fridausi was dead and that that was his corpse.

Now the day arrived when that magnificent monarch too must quit this world. His eyes were opened to the fact that the wealth he had acquired by quenching the light[3] of

[1] A *fataḥ-nāma* is a written proclamation of victory sent to all governors by the chief ruler. [2] Direct narration in the original.

[3] This metaphor does not seem apt. To quench the light of a family should mean to kill the eldest son.

thousands of families, has all to be abandoned. He was sixty-three years of age when he fell ill. When no hope of life remained to him, he ordered his stewards and treasurers to bring before his eyes, the bags of rupees, ashrafīs, ornaments, jewels, rich suits of clothes, royal raiment, and all the rare and wonderful things he had collected. The court-yard of the palace was furnished with them and made into a museum. The treasurer kept on showing him the things, one by one, and he kept on looking at them with eyes full of regret, shedding bitter tears the while.

The next day he ordered that all his private elephants, horses, and camels should be paraded with all their trappings and ornaments and gorgeous (glittering) saddle-cloths. Maḥmūd was brought in an open litter (*nālkī*) and gazed at them for long, and then returned to the palace weeping and wailing. None of his brave chiefs or faithful adherents who had been his comrades in his perilous wars, could offer him companionship now. At last he departed from the world, empty-handed as he had entered it.

3. ẒAHĪR-UD-DĪN BĀBUR.[1]

On the death of Maḥmūd his family began to go down,[2] till at length the Panjāb, and Ghaznī too, were lost to it. Other Muslim dynasties arose and conquered many big provinces of India, and established themselves at Delhi; and, after ruling several generations, departed from this world. For a long time these dynasties ruled till (*ki*) Amīr Tīmūr[3] came from Turkistan, and, laying waste the Panjāb, reached Delhi, looted it, and massacred the inhabitants; but he came like a storm and departed like a whirlwind. After his departure, another dynasty rose in Delhi and came to an end. Another was

[1] *Ẓahīr*, "helper." *Bābur*, and not *Babar*, is, I am informed by Dr. Denison Ross, the correct Turki pronunciation, a point established by the rhyme in Turki verse.

[2] *Zawāl*, decline of the sun, etc.

[3] *Tīmūr-i lang* ("Timur the lame")=Tamerlane.

ruling when King Bābur, a descendant of Tīmūr, arose in Turkistan, and marched at the head of an army into India. It was he who founded the Chaghatā,ī dynasty. Now, please, (*zarā*) listen to an account of Bābur.

He was twelve years of age when he ascended the throne and ruled with great energy.[1] If we peruse his story we cannot fail to be astonished.

At one moment we see him famous (*lit.* with kettledrums[2] sounding) and ruling over millions, at another fleeing through mountains and forests and finding no place to hide.[3] For twenty-two years he wielded the sword in the North, but Fortune (*iqbāl*[4]) did not favour him. At length he thought of India, and claimed it as his hereditary country because Amīr Tīmūr had (has) taken it by the sword.

Sulṭān Ibrāhīm, who was then ruling in Delhi, was cruel, careless, and ease-loving, and incapable of managing the country. Several Amīrs of the Darbār sent word to Bābur to come (*bulā-bhejnā*). As for Bābur, he was watching for such an opportunity (*mauqa'*). He started at the head of an army, and fighting and skirmishing advanced up to the plain of Panipat and encamped there. Ibrāhīm came out of Delhi to meet him, at the head of more than a hundred thousand men, and a thousand war elephants. Bābur had come with only twelve thousand, and with that force he opposed him. Certainly he had artillery, which up till the present had never cut up the battle-fields of India. Well, it was early morning when the battle began and the fight was hot till past noon. At last Ibrāhīm was slain and Bābur was victorious. This was such an important battle that its fame has lasted even up till to-day. After this, he won[5] several other battles by which his sovereign power (*salṭanat*) was firmly established (*jam-jānā*).

1 The author has got a little mixed here.

2 *Naqqāra* means lit. the *naqqār-khāna* or *naubat-khāna*, the drums beaten at dawn and sunset, at the gate of the palace.

3 These two historical facts are stated in the wrong order.

4 What is the difference between *iqbāl* and *qismat* ?

5 Note idiom.

Although Bābur sometimes treated his enemies with great cruelty, still he quickly relented (*narm ho-jānā*). He was very courageous and never lost his head in the presence of danger, or lost heart (*himmat hārnā*) under misfortune. In one battle his Sardārs got nervous and upset, seeing the numbers (*kas̤rat*) of the enemy, and advised the abandonment of India. To make matters even worse an astrologer had just arrived from Turkistan, who said that his science too taught him that the enemy would be victorious in the impending (*is*) victory. At this his adherents became even more upset than before, but Bābur was not turned aside from his intention (*apne irāde par jamā-rahā*). When he gained the victory, he sent for the astrologer; and, first putting him to shame (*sharmānā*), he threatened him a bit, but at last he gave him a big reward saying, "Now depart from this place."

Bābur was enterprising (*'ālī himmat*) and magnanimous. He readily pardoned rebellious relations and servants alike, when they came to him repentantly (*sharminda hokar ānā*). He was a straightforward Turk, alike inside and out; what was in his heart was on his tongue. He never had recourse to treachery and deceit. He was just. Hence he won a good reputation. Once a caravan of merchants came from some far place into his district. In the hills they encountered such terrible cold[1] that all perished but two. Bābur had the whole of their goods extricated, and carefully stored, and sent messages to their country. When the real heirs arrived, he handed over to them every thread (*tār-tār*).

Though in war he thought hardship no hardship, yet no sooner was he free from war than he began to enjoy life (*zindagī se ḥaz̤z̤ uṭhānā*) as though he had nothing else in the world to do but amuse himself.

He was passionately fond (*—kā 'āshiq*) of nature, and delighted in flowers and gardens, and the verdure of Spring. He used to wander over green hills or sit with his comrades on the banks of streams: they drank wine and sang odes. He himself

[1] For *balā* and *g̱ẖaẓab*, *vide* "Hindustani Manual," pages 54 and 69.

was a poet, and we have a Turki *Dīwān* [1] of him. Sometimes he composed (*kahnā*) in Persian. He has written his autobiography, from which it appears that he never omitted to notice every little thing he saw, wherever he went. In one passage he marvels at the people of India and says, "They are a people strangely lacking in taste, for, if by chance they encamp on the bank of a river, they will pitch their tents facing the other way; the charms of Nature make not the least impression on them."

A strange story is told about the death of Bābur. He had been out of sorts (*'alīl*)) for some days and at that time his son Humāyūn too was very ill. Many remedies were tried without avail. At last someone said to the king, in an assembly of learned and religious people (*buzurg*), that learned men among the ancients have written with regard to such an occasion that the most valued object should be offered as 'a sacrifice to avert misfortune' (*ṣadaqa*), and the Almighty then petitioned. Bābur replied, "To Humāyūn I am the most valued object. I will sacrifice my life for his." His companions remonstrated with him urging that the meaning of the saying of the ancients was that the most costly article of property should be given, and hence that he should 'sacrifice' the rare and priceless diamond belonging to the prince. The King said, "No article of worldly goods can be the price of Humāyūn; only my life can be sacrificed for him." In short, having prayed to God, he circled [2] round the prince's bedstead three times, and thinking that he had now taken his sickness upon himself,[3] said, "I have taken it, I have taken it." In short Bāhur's illness increased rapidly while Humāyūn's sickness began to decline, so much so that the son got up from bed while the father went and prostrated himself on his death-bed.

1 *Pūrā* means his *dīwān* or 'collected poetical works' are found complete.

2 And so took his calamities upon himself. This is a Hindu custom as well. It is also customary in Persia and Arabia, but seems to be dying out.

3 Direct narration.

4. THE DEVOTION OF THE NURSE.

The Chaghatā,ī dynasty were often at war with the Rājpūts. The Rājpūts were far inferior in point of numbers to the Mughal army, still they did not fear to fight to preserve the freedom of their country; and to preserve their honour they fought like lions. Many stories are told of their intrepid bravery (*lit.* bravery and intrepidity). To say nothing of the men, many great deeds were performed by their women. In boldness and faithfulness, they fully equalled their men. In Rājpūtānā, Rānā Udai Singh was the Rājā of Mewāṛ. His story is a strange one. Just see how in those days both men and women were devoted to their masters (*āqā*), and how faithful they were in the time of trouble.

Prince Udai Singh and his very small foster-brother were sleeping in some out-building of the palace. A woman, the nurse of the prince and the mother of another child, was sitting with her loved little ones. On one side was a basket of fruit and the remains of a meal. Both the children had eaten and were asleep. Suddenly the sound of the weeping and wailing of the Rānīs reached her. The nurse guessed that some terrible calamity had befallen them. She was sitting disturbed waiting to see what would happen, when suddenly (*itne meṅ*) a servant came to clear away the remains of the meal. She asked him if all were well. He replied, "How can it be well? His enemies have done for the Rānā." As soon as the nurse heard this she was rivetted to the spot.[1] Terror so overcame her that had one cut her (Aorist; were you to cut her), no blood would have been found in her body. With her fear came the thought, "When the Rānā has been killed, how will the prince escape? They will kill him too in a few moments. By some plan his life must be saved." But there was no time for deliberation, for the danger was that the door might open at any moment to admit those butchers. The

[1] *Lit.* "her hands and feet swelled," *i.e.*, she was unable to move (from *fear* or grief).

prince lay asleep. Slowly the nurse took him in her arms and laid him in the fruit basket and covered him with leaves. The child slept heedlessly on. The nurse said to the servant, "Take this basket out of the fort," and then she quickly placed [1] her own child in the place of the prince.

The servant had only just gone out (*nikalā hī thā*) when the tyrant arrived, his hands dyed red with the Rānā's blood. He had dertermined to kill the prince, and asked the nurse where Udai Singh was. The faithful nurse had lost all power of speech; she pointed to her son. Although maternal affection overcame her, still she allowed no harm to come to the prince. No sooner had she pointed than the butcher despatched her beloved child with his dagger. The mother looked on all the time (*dekhtī rahī*) and neither uttered a word nor shed a tear for fear lest she should betray her secret.

The faithful nurse made a (that) sacrifice, which makes our hair stand on end; but the prince was saved. He grew up (*jawān hū,ā*) and one of his sons Partāb Singh turned out such a hero that he offered continued opposition to Akbar.

5. THE BRAVERY OF PARTĀB SINGH.

By the fidelity of the nurse Udai Singh's life was saved. He remained hidden for a long time, and the fact was known to only a very few of the Rājpūts. After some years, it became known that the heir to the throne was (is) alive. People had suffered much at the hands of Bānbīr. The Sardārs combined (*milkar*) and removed him from the throne, and placed the crown on the head of Udai Singh. Sad to relate, he had no royal quality nor any of the bravery of the Rājpūts. In those days Akbar Shāh, the grandson of Bābur, had ascended the throne of Delhi and became king of India. He had defeated all the enemies who had fought with him, and had turned his attention to Rajputana. Chittoṛ was the capital of Mewāṛ, and there there was a very strong and famous fortress. Akbar be-

[1] *Liṭā-diyā.*

sieged it. Udai Singh abandoned it and fled, but the Rājpūt chiefs remained to defend it. They fought without any regard for their lives. When no hope remained, nine Rānīs, five Princesses, and very many women of the palace turned themselves into a heap of burnt ashes. The Rājpūts opened the gates and came out sword in hand, and were cut to pieces on the spot. Udai Singh, after abandoning Chittoṛ, settled in the Arbalī hills. He built a palace for his residence and founded a city around it, and that is the Udaipūr which is still the capital of Mewāṛ. When he died, his son Partāb ascended the throne. This is that Partāb whose name is still mentioned with pride by the Rājpūts.

At that time he had none of the accompaniments of royalty. Daily defeats had broken the spirit of his relations, but in his veins the true (*wuhī*) Rājpūt blood continued to surge. He used to say, "When a sword is in one's hands, is the release of Chittoṛ a great matter? I will maintain the honour of the Rājpūts and keep alive the name of my ancestors."

He had to face a powerful monarch like Akbar, who had all the resources of the Indian Empire at his command and up till that time no such wise politic (*bā tadbīr*) king had ever sat on the throne of India. Several Rājpūt Rājās had suffered defeat at his hands, and most of them had submitted to him (*lit.* obeyed him) and had been well treated. Their territories had been restored to them but they remained tributary. From some of their royal families Akbar took wives. By this policy (*in tadbīroṅ se*) he had bound to him many of the Rājās, but Partāb refused to acknowledge him and could not bear to see the freedom of his country taken away. For this reason other Rājpūt Rājās became enraged with him and came out to fight him. That man of great heart for twenty-five years sometimes fought in the field, and sometimes took to the hills. Akbar even admitted his bravery and determination. He much wished to conclude an honourable peace with him, and even sent an offer of marriage, but he refused to accept such a disgrace and gave back a straight answer to everything. Even to-day his victories are on Rājpūt tongues. Amongst them,[1] was the battle of Haldī Ghāṭ in which he escaped falling into his enemies' hands by a strange circumstance:—

Akbar's son, Salīm, taking a large army of veterans and heavy artillery, was encamped in the field of Haldī Ghāṭ. Partāb with twenty-two thousand Rājpūts opposed him and stopped him in a pass. The battle was hot. Partāb was mounted on his high-bred horse named Chaṭak. Wherever the fight was hottest, there he appeared on his horse. At last cutting his way through the king's horse and foot, he reached the Prince who was in the very centre of the army directing the fight. His death seemed certain but he was sitting in a box-hauda covered with plates of steel and hence he escaped. It was useless[2] for Partāb to try to kill him with a spear. The well-bred horse aided its rider. The painters of the time have depicted this scene as follows: His horse is rearing up on end, with one foot resting on the elephant, and he is about to strike the prince with his spear.

Salīm's life was in danger but his calamity fell on the poor mahāwat, and the elephant became infuriated and ran away, and bore off Salīm with it; but still the Rājpūts and the king's troops continued the fight with energy. Partāb received seven wounds. He was three times surrounded and escaped; the last time he was very nearly done for. Seeing the state of affairs the Sardār of Jhālāwār wished somehow or other to save Partāb even at imminent risk to his own life. He took the standard of Partāb, *i.e.*, a sun-flower,[3] and drew away from the fight. The king's troops thought (*lit.* knew) that he was[4] Partāb; all burst away in his direction and the heat of the fight was suddenly transferred there (*laṛā,ī kā zor udhar jā-paṛā*). The luckless Sardār with all his comrades was slain, but Partāb got

[1] This appears to have been a *defeat* for Partāb, not a victory.

[2] Note this difficult idiom.

[3] *Sūraj-mukhī* is a sun-flower, but I am not sure that it is the correct translation here.

[4] Direct narration: *Partāb yihī hai.*

clean away from the spot where he was surrounded. The Rājpūts fought desperately but in vain;[1] of twenty-two thousand *jawāns* only eight thousand were left alive.

Partāb now left the field without a companion. He was faint from wounds. This faithful horse Chaṭak was under him. Two Muslim Sardārs recognised him and gave chase. Their horses were about to[2] overtake him when a hill nālā came in the way. The courageous Chaṭak flew it clean and his enemies were left, but this was a respite (*muhlat*) of but a few moments, for his adversaries came out of the *nālā* and again pursued. Chaṭak too, after a whole day's work, was done up and was also wounded like his rider: his strength began to go. Partāb had no hope of escape left. His enemies were toiling after him and by the clatter of their horses' feet on the hard stones it was evident they were quite close. Suddenly a Rājpūt voice reached his ears, "Oh rider on the iron-grey!" He looked round and saw there was only one pursuer and that he was his brother Sakat.

Sakat, annoyed at something, had left his home while a boy; he was so estranged that he had become disgusted with his country as well as with his brother. He had joined Akbar's army and up till then had fought against his own people; but now, having witnessed his brother's intrepid bravery,[3] his heart was filled with emotion. He saw two enemies pursuing him, while he the pursued, and his horse, were both wounded. Brotherly affection could not bear the sight, and he rushed at the two pursuers and killed them (*mār-girānā*), and so, after a lifetime (*'umr*), the two brothers opened their arms and embraced. At this moment Chaṭak, worn out, dropped, and dropping died. Sakat gave his brother his own horse, and merely saying "If an opportunity offers I will come and see you again," he took his leave.

1 This is a colloquial use of *nā-ḥaqq* which properly means "unjustly."

2 For this meaning of *chāhnā vide* "Hindustani Manual," pp. 71 (*a*) and 74 (*b*).

3 Translate by two substantives.

The king's army were every moment expecting to see the sawārs' return with Partāb bound. They were surprised to see Sakat returning alone and took him straight before the Prince. The Prince said, "What has happened to my Sardārs?" The reply was, "Partāb killed them and got off: my own horse too was killed; I have ridden back (*chaṛh-kar āyā hūṅ*) on one of the Sirdār's horses." Salīm did not credit this. He took him aside and said, "Tell me the whole truth. If you have done wrong I will forgive you." Sakat related the whole of the circumstances. Salīm too, a man of his word, did[1] nothing to Sakat, but dismissed him from his army. Sakat went off and joined his brother.

[1] Note this meaning of *kahnā*. *Vide* also "Hindustani Manual," p. 43 (c).

END.

CPSIA information can be obtained
at www.ICGtesting.com
Printed in the USA
BVHW070821040219
539400BV00034B/2407/P